Hell's Mouth

By

A P Bateman

Author contact: authorapbateman@gmail.com
Facebook: @authorapbateman
Website: apbateman.com

Also by A P Bateman

The Alex King Series

The Contract Man

Lies and Retribution

Shadows of Good Friday

The Rob Stone Series

The Ares Virus

The Town

The Island

For the used and abused, the pawns in those wicked games of the few, who affect the lives of so many. Those whose lives have no value to the people who need them, to the people who would take them. We will win, they have already lost.

For the other three in "The Four Family"

Thank you…

1

Tell me when you see it...

Those had been his final words. Not deathbed style. Nothing as dramatic or theatrical as that. But he had been adamant. He had told him half a story and given him the means and time and opportunity to discover the other half. It had been typical of Anderson. He had not wanted the man's opinion jaded in any way. Simply outlined what he had seen; but the truth, the ultimate end to the tale, was for him to discover.

Ross O'Bryan put down the telephone. He would know who his new boss would be soon enough. He felt numb at the news, but death was an old and constant companion. He had spent enough time with it, knew the processes of grief only too well. In his darkest hours, he did not fear death, nor shied from its path. Outside forces had contributed, but ultimately death was a face he no longer feared to stare into. Occasionally he goaded it, stared coldly and dared it to make its move. It had made for a flat-line in both career and love. He was unbreakable. He was uncontrollable. Untameable. And that meant that with the replacement of his long-time boss, he would most likely be unemployable. He was a crisis man. The man you wanted on board when the toughest choices had to be made, when it counted. But crisis men were like tethered animals. They only truly lived when they were free.

Fifty-nine days…

The longest period since the clock turned back and the marker read zero. His heart fluttered and his stomach tensed. He could feel a sudden rush in his chest cavity as the blood surged quicker through his veins. He started to ball his fists as he walked out of Anderson's study and into the lounge. Anderson had kept a crystal decanter of brandy in the study and the temptation was behind him now. He had looked at the decanter, its amber contents glistening in the late afternoon sun which had shone brightly through the windows. The close proximity of the water had seemed to intensify the light, given it an added quality of brightness he seldom saw, or perhaps noticed in London.

The entire south wall of the lounge had been replaced by glass doors and the view spoke for itself. The creek was almost at high-tide and the water was the deepest blue, pooling to black in the shadows of the trees on the other side. It was late summer, the final weeks where the next front of cold weather spelled the end of the season and the beginning of autumn.

The body of water this far up the creek wasn't popular with paddle boarders or kayakers. It was shallow and held on to the flat bed of mud and grass for all but three-quarter tide. Lower down the creek at

Point Geddon, less than a mile distant, there would be hordes of children, clad in brightly coloured wetsuits, jumping off the jetty and into the deep water. There would be kayaks and other craft paddling through the moorings as the last weeks of ideal boating conditions were exploited, and sailors started preparing their boats for hauling out of the water for the long winter months.

Across the water lay an old wooden jetty. It was all but hidden from view by a large fallen tree which must have become snagged, or sucked into the mud, because it hadn't moved for the entire week. Each time the tide partially submerged it, but still it did not move. The absence of leaves would indicate that it had not fallen this summer. It looked to have been there for years. Perhaps it had taken root in the mud. O'Bryan did not know about such things, lacked the care to Google it, but he reasoned that it was not in the way of the tiny jetty, nor the rest of the river, so its presence was of no consequence.

O'Bryan stepped into the open doorway and leaned on the warm glass. Birds skimmed the surface of the water, and some kind of large black and white bird was ducking down repeatedly and reappearing twenty or thirty-feet further down the creek each time. It seemed to be following a line. O'Bryan figured there was food there. Perhaps shrimp. But what did he know? He couldn't have said whether it was a cormorant or a duck.

He stepped out and felt the sun on his face. It was hovering between late afternoon and early evening. Another hour until dusk. The sun was warm and the water looked inviting enough to swim in. He put the thought out of his mind. A bad experience, a trauma he supposed, had left him with little desire to swim. It was too soon. The close proximity of the creek had left him feeling anxious, but he reasoned he had control over it. He just had to stay on dry land. He had been a champion swimmer a lifetime ago, and a water polo player at university. The sport had shaped him, broadened his shoulders, trimmed his waist and left him with an athletic build, even when he no longer trained. It saddened him that another part of his life was over and he was left with nothing but regret and distant memories. He seemed to be following a pattern throughout life. Or maybe it was just the way it went when you got older, crossed into the uncertainty of middle-age.

The warmth of the sun did nothing to lift his spirits. The call had been swift, but mainly because he was at a loss what to say. What did you say to a woman whose husband has just died? O'Bryan counted Anderson as one of his closest friends, even if he had been his boss since he arrived in the department. He hadn't known the man had been suffering with cancer; wouldn't even have guessed. But that was what the man had been like. Anderson wouldn't want pity or sorrow or awkward silences in a conversation. It struck O'Bryan that the man's wife hadn't known either, although it didn't surprise him of the man. He was tough and would want to be remembered that way. He hadn't even looked sick, but there were a few tell-tale signs upon reflection. Weight loss, colour, absence. But all handled like typical Anderson. *Diet. Need a bloody holiday. Busy on an investigation, hush-hush stuff.* He wondered whether Anderson had helped himself along, found a way out before the suffering reduced him as a man. He would have known a few methods that would not have been obvious. Or maybe he had got his wife to help him, and she was a little off during the conversation because of fear or guilt or regret. He made a note to put his oar in if he heard anything on the grapevine, anything to give her an easier ride. *If* he had a job to go back to.

O'Bryan needed a beer. A cold glass in the setting sun, a toast to his departed friend, his mentor and his boss. Just one bottle. Frosted, quenching, but wholly unforgiving. There were some bottles of something German in the back of the fridge. He could imagine the sound of the bottle top spinning off and hitting the marble counter, hear the fizz of the beer as it frothed, see the tiny bubbles pop and burst in the air above the rim.

He could taste it...

Before he knew it, he was running. He kicked the wooden gate open, his pace barely slowing as he joined the well-trodden path along the bank of the creek. He hadn't run for more than two-months. Not since before his accident. Or incident. Incident would best describe it. He shook his head, clearing the memory. Focus. Focus on the pace, his breath, his stride. Think about anything else but the bottle, anything else but the empty bottle that invariably always led to another.

Fifty-nine days...

O'Bryan knew the problem. He had been inactive for too long. He needed a crutch. Something to take a hold of him, his mind and body. His soul. Anderson had seen that. He had known what a task it would be for him to take a full two-months away from his desk, his patch. He had given him the chance of a break, but one with purpose. One he was most suited to. But what? O'Bryan cursed the man for being so cryptic. There had been the newspaper clippings from the national press and a good deal of reports from the *Westbriton* when the nationals moved swiftly onto the next story. And there had been the copies of the reports he had pulled. Anderson had clout, that much was obvious. He had increased O'Bryan's leave and postponed his psychoanalyst programmes after the initial inquiry. He knew O'Bryan needed something practical to concentrate on, and no amount of therapy was going to change what had happened. He also knew that O'Bryan hid a condition that would have cost him his job. Analysts had a habit and ability to unearth more than was good for their patient.

Anderson had been the one person O'Bryan could count on, and now the man was dead. And with it, O'Bryan's hopes of continuing with the investigation. Without Anderson, it was as good as dead in the water.

Dead in the water...

O'Bryan stopped running and stared at the water. The tide was moving rapidly, like a walking escalator at an airport. There was a piece of driftwood coming in with it and it gave a sense of perspective of how fast the tide was moving. He knew it went out faster. Or he might have made that up. Either way, it seemed obvious to him that the pull would be stronger than the push. Especially in calm conditions with no storm surge.

He watched a medium-sized fishing boat coming in. It was powered by an in-built diesel engine that sounded as if it had seen better days, around fifty-years ago, and housed a substantial cabin on the foredeck. O'Bryan could see two men at the helm. One rolled a cigarette and the other raised his finger, covered his left nostril and shot-gunned his nose, a spray of snot hitting the water. They glanced at him, but O'Bryan looked away, and from the corner of his eye, they both looked uninterested as they piloted the boat around an exposed mud bank and onwards up the creek. The rear section of the deck was stacked with two types of lobster or crab pots. Rounded ones that looked as if they were made from wicker and larger square metal cages. Huge coils of rope seemed to pack them in. There were plastic crates staked alongside.

Anderson had been quite specific. Tonight was the second time and date in the letter. O'Bryan had missed the first time, last week. He had met up with a woman that he had initially met on his first night in the local pub. He felt bad missing the time and date, but Anderson could be a dick sometimes. He had felt obliged to come down to Cornwall, as though it were an order rather than a suggestion, although he had been quite entitled to his time off from work, in light of what had happened. This had been Anderson's family home, or at least one of them. His commander had referred to it as the *Hemingway House*, because of its likeness to the writer Ernest Hemingway's house in Key West, Florida. Strangely, it did not look out of place, predominately because of the types of house which had sprung up over the past decade or so. This was an affluent area, one of second homes and holiday lets, and the plots were being bought up and old houses knocked down in favour of newly built chrome, glass and expensively weathered oak constructions. *Hemingway House* was modern, but chic. It added a touch of class to the area, where only money remained. Money and class were not inextricably linked.

The date had gone well. They had picked up where they had left off, but without the cluster of regulars heckling them at *The Smuggler's Rest*. They had met for cocktails in Truro and gone on to eat at a favourable Italian chain restaurant. O'Bryan had stuck rigidly to the crutch of his car. If he was driving, it was socially unacceptable to drink, especially within their age group. Besides, a taxi back to Point Geddon and Barlooe Creek beyond was a ludicrous proposition to most. The myriad of roads, the hills and narrow turnings to get out to the creek. Situated past Mylor, a taxi would cost almost as much as the meal itself. In his mind, at least. With that, the cocktails had been 'mocktails' and a simple lime and soda went well with the meal instead of chilled Italian beer. There may be a talk about his drinking later, but this wasn't first date conversation. The gap in both age and dynamic had taken a downwards turn when Sarah had suggested a club. O'Bryan was nudging forty and it showed in his panic at the prospect of dancing in a loud and crowded club with a thirty-year-old who would pass for early twenties. The sincerity and confidence of the idea was put into context, when they arrived and discovered the club had been closed down for a considerable length of time. Sarah looked like she felt a little foolish, and O'Bryan could tell, along with snippets of

14

conversation throughout the night, that she did not get out as much as she liked to pretend. He doubted she got out at all. And that meant there had to be a reason. Something she had not disclosed, something she had purposely avoided.

It was the detective in him. The role never left him. Not even when it had cost him his wife and child. But that hadn't been the only reason.

Fifty-nine days…

He glanced at his watch. The sun was below the furthest-most headland towards Restronguet. The timing would be right. He turned and ran back to the house. There was the occasional dog walker, who said, "Good evening…" or nodded a greeting. He could not get used to it. People actually *spoke* to strangers down here. In London they'd call the police, because you would clearly have escaped from some sort of institution if you behaved in such a way.

The boat's rough-sounding engine belied its speed and O'Bryan had to run a good pace to catch up with it as he rounded the point and drew close to Barlooe Creek. The *Hemingway House* looked as splendid as ever, but the light was low here and he knew that there may not be enough light to watch what happened next.

Breathless and tentative, he ran through the doors and into the lounge. Anderson had appreciated ornithology and kept a pair of Zeiss binoculars on the bookshelf next to the glass doors. O'Bryan picked them up. They were a good magnification and a series of symbols on the side of the frame indicated they were suitable for low light conditions, as well as their degree of magnification and width of angle. There were no lights on in the house and he stood a few feet back to remain invisible. He raised the glasses and watched the boat. It skirted the fallen tree, throttled backwards, and suddenly O'Bryan could see how significant the tree was. It all but hid the boat from view. There were enough branches to disrupt the silhouette of the vessel, combined with the trees on the shoreline and the ambiance of dusk, the boat had disappeared. O'Bryan knew this was what Anderson had meant for him to see. The time, the date, the location. But why? Why would a commander in Special Branch have an interest in this? These men could be fishing, or poaching from the nearby estate. There were deer all over that headland. O'Bryan had heard gunshots the night before. But this was the country, not London and nobody seemed to bat an eyelid. He had mentioned it at The Smuggler's Rest, and one of the men at the bar had offered him some rabbits the next time he went out.

The men on the boat could be bringing in cigarettes and alcohol to escape duty. A questionable activity, and one that no police officer would ignore, but merely a tip off to the local constabulary would be action enough. Why had Anderson seen fit to offer his house to a recuperating officer? What wasn't

O'Bryan seeing? He kept his eyes on the area where the boat had moored. He could no longer see the tree, and only guessed at where the boat was, but he could see a figure on the jetty. One of the men for sure. Then, two more figures. No, three. Varying sizes, perhaps indicating either different sexes or ages. O'Bryan closed his eyes for a moment. There were the reports, the newspaper articles. He opened his eyes and pressed them closer to the binoculars in vain. He strained his eyes, moved the focus. He took them away and checked the magnification. There was a dial. He was on seven and it went to ten. Perfect. There was a switch on the top of the frame simply marked 'on' and 'off'. It had to be better if you turned it on. He raised them and looked again. For a fleeting moment he saw a figure looking back at him, a set of binoculars raised. The light in the room illuminated him, cast his silhouette in the open doorway. He visibly jumped.

"What on earth are you doing?" Sarah asked. She walked in, carrying two brown paper bags and an aroma of Chinese food wafting in with her.

"Switch off the light!" he yelled. She looked at him incredulously. She was not accustomed to being shouted at. Either that, or she had been once and had now drawn a line in the sand. He suspected the latter. "The light, the bloody light!" he yelled again. He turned back as she tutted loudly and switched it off. He raised the binoculars. The man on the distant jetty had gone. O'Bryan felt the tiny hairs rise on the nape of his neck. He had a sinking feeling that he had witnessed something that someone would go to great lengths to make sure he hadn't.

2

Seven weeks earlier
London

DI Ross O'Bryan studied the photo in his lap. He checked the man walking towards him, there was no beard, and his hair was cropped short instead of his usual long, greasy strands, bordering on dreadlocks. The man was thinner too. Drawn in, gaunt. Was it him? He'd been this close before. Sat opposite him for three days of questioning. Sat across the courtroom from him for two-months during the trial. He'd been forced to watch the man walk away then. But not now. Not today. With just ten paces between them, he folded the photograph so that only the eyes remained. He focused for a moment, then stared directly into the man's face. Two seconds, and he was gone. Past the car and walking away with his back to the wing mirror. It was all he needed. Those eyes were the same. Like the eyes of a shark. Dark and lifeless.

He lifted the radio, just enough to capture his voice, not raising it into view for the rest of the people crossing the bridge to see. "Control, Bravo Delta Two," he said, clearly and in control despite the building adrenalin within. "Positive ID, repeat, positive ID."

"Bravo Delta Two, confirmed, positive ID. All units, standby, standby. Sit rep on SCO19?"

"SCO19. Four minutes."

"Speed up."

"Control. Bravo Delta Two, I'm in position," O'Bryan interjected when the net was clear.

"Denied."

"Control, I'm right here!" O'Bryan snapped. "He's got the look; he's praying as he walks! Whatever he's going to do, he's going to do it now!"

"Denied, DI O'Bryan. Wait out!"

Shaved, hair trimmed, washed and presentable, wide-eyed and mouthing a prayer, almost in a meditative state. It didn't get more imminent than that. O'Bryan opened the door of the van and swung his wiry six-foot frame out onto the pavement. He kept the radio down by his side. He could see the man from behind. He had a shuffle going on, like he was rocking to a beat as he walked. Which indeed he was. But it went with the chant he was mouthing, nothing musical, merely the constant reciting of a near-silent prayer.

Ahead of the man, O'Bryan could see the gathering of children. A school outing, the children holding leaflets, gathered around a brass plaque. William Wordsworth's poem of Westminster Bridge. The teacher leading the talk was standing with her back to the river. Parents or teaching assistants stood nearby, cordoning off the children as they watched and listened. She had a sheet of paper in her hands and she cleared her throat before speaking. Had O'Bryan been closer, he would have heard:

"Earth has not anything to show more fair:
Dull would he be of soul who could pass by
A sight so touching in its majesty:
This City now doth like a garment wear
The beauty of the morning; silent, bare,
Ships, towers, domes, theatres, and temples lie
Open unto the fields, and to the sky;
All bright and glittering in the smokeless air.
Never did sun more beautifully steep
In his first splendour valley, rock, or hill;
Ne'er saw I, never felt, a calm so deep!
The river glideth at his own sweet will:
Dear God! the very houses seem asleep;
And all that mighty heart is lying still!"

The teacher continued to talk and the children listened. Passers-by paused and nodded. The bridge had seen a terrorist atrocity when self-styled terrorist and Islamic extremist Khalid Masood killed four and injured more than fifty people when he drove down the pavement at over seventy-miles-per-hour and crashed his hire car outside The Palace of Westminster and callously murdered PC Keith Palmer on 22nd March 2017.

DI Ross O'Bryan was sure the bridge was about to see another attack. They had been lucky with the intelligence. Social media was being monitored constantly, but Abhim Maqsood had been careless. He had not friended a person, but a picture, a story, a social invention. He had requested the friendship of a person who didn't exist, from a computer and server in a place that did. GCHQ. A team of operators trawling the net for an 'in'. The software and telephone recognition system, known as ECHELON had picked up Maqsood six months previous, and not just one, but three times. Maqsood was targeted and a number of attempts to insert a cyber-spy into his network was rebuked. But then came the break the intelligence operatives at Cheltenham had prayed for, Maqsood sent a friend request to a ghost account and they had him. They didn't pounce, keeping him waiting a week to be accepted, but then it was on. That person who appealed to him was ingeniously inserted into his internet usage. Someone who came up as a suggested friend because of other ghost accounts he had as so called friends. Maqsood could see the posts, did not know that the two-hundred friends the ghost account displayed were all GCHQ accounts and 'legends' and it was not long before the extremist rhetoric played to Abhim Maqsood and hooked him in. Open messages were sent, with each end describing what they wanted to do and achieve in the name of Allah. Human rights lawyers would argue entrapment and coercion, but the accounts were filtering enough 'real' people, and GCHQ were confident, that with help and cooperation from MI5, that they could sever the line and keep Maqsood's social media trail natural to all who would later inspect it. Besides, they were the country's communication intelligence service and were protected by joint intelligence and the terrorism act. The truth was, the extremists were there, they sometimes needed bolstering and nurturing, encouraging even, to step up and commit their act of terrorism. Better it was the intelligence services than an extremist cleric or Imam where the trail would remain undetected.

As an officer of Special Branch, DI Ross O'Bryan was part of the joint operation with MI5, working on the intel handed over by GCHQ – a non-field operational service. The role of Special Branch in an operation such as this, was to make MI5's arrest. SCO19, the specialist armed police unit of highly-trained officers was on hand to provide armed support. The arrest would be hard, armed officers surrounding Maqsood and eliminating the threat. O'Bryan and his team would read the rights, so to speak and MI5 would accompany Special Branch officers in the interview. Only it hadn't worked out that way. Maqsood had given the surveillance team the slip, the officers were dispersed all over the city and had only just relocated Maqsood by chance. O'Bryan had cut through the traffic by a devious route and made it to the bridge. SCO19 were in transit from what was initially confirmed as the target area, a shopping centre situated on the other side of the river. Now that O'Bryan had got the second eyes-on and confirmed a positive ID, the target made sense. Maqsood was a former colleague of Khalid Masood and Westminster Bridge seemed a fitting location to rein terror once more.

O'Bryan broke into a jog, keeping his eyes on Maqsood. His pace slowed and he fumbled with his jacket. It was a hot day, but the jacket had been noted, profiling had indicated that Maqsood would be operating alone. They knew there would be something under the jacket. Maqsood's browser history was of suicide vests and bomb-making. SCO19 had been made aware of this in the briefing. Standard operating procedure of taking shots at the target's central body mass was being changed by the advent of suicide vests. Israeli officers now only attempted head shots. The practise was becoming the same for British forces. They would ultimately have to make their own call, but the officers had each come onto their shift knowing that if they needed to fire upon Maqsood, then extreme prejudice protocols would be required.

Maqsood stopped at the group of school children. O'Bryan was sprinting now. Maqsood pulled his jacket off to reveal a vest, but this was no suicide vest. There were two short handled kanjar knives, or Arabian daggers, strapped to the man's back. The vest was a bullet-proof or stab-proof vest, and slashes made in the top layer of material acted as sheaths for the kanjar knives. He drew them swiftly, both blades were approximately fourteen inches long, curved and had wickedly pointed tips. Maqsood slashed them through the air and the first person, a parent or teaching assistant, fell to the floor, partially decapitated. He did not wait to look at his handiwork; merely kept slashing. The full horror of what was happening took moments for the onlookers to comprehend, in which time, Maqsood had felled another adult and a small child. People screamed and ran in both directions, and an oncoming crowd soon blocked O'Bryan's view of the terrible scene. O'Bryan pushed the terrified people out of the way as he barged onwards.

Maqsood had a group of children cornered at a buttress. There was terror on their faces and the sound of screaming came from every direction. Amid the chaos, a teenaged boy had stopped walking and was filming the scene. His presence seemed surreal, voyeuristic in the extreme. O'Bryan could hear approaching sirens and the noise of the screaming was dying down as people ran far enough away to safety. He reached the first casualty, but he could already see that they were dead. The next body was that of a child, equally as far gone as the first body. No hope.

Maqsood stood above a woman who was sobbing and crawling into the road. She was the teacher who had recited the poem, and she was bleeding seriously from slashes to her arms, legs and shoulders. She looked to have put up a fight, and O'Bryan could see she must have been defending a group of children huddled between the wall and buttress of the bridge. Maqsood kept the group of children in sight, watching their faces as he drove the tip of the dagger into the woman's back. She shuddered and gasped, her legs shook and as he pulled the blade back out, she relaxed and lay still.

O'Bryan barrelled into Maqsood at an astonishing closing speed and took the man to the ground. Maqsood was winded for a moment, but suddenly started lashing out with the blade in his left hand. He had dropped the other blade onto the pavement with a clatter. An onlooker stepped over the knife and hustled away, like it was a good opportunity and he would not be late for his appointment after all.

O'Bryan felt the slash against his shoulder, felt the knock of the blade upon bone. It did not hurt, but he knew that he had been wounded. Maqsood was getting to his feet and reaching for the other dagger. O'Bryan rolled to put some distance between them, kept glancing behind him to keep Maqsood in his vision. He could feel the slash now. It burned and froze all at once. Maqsood was back on his feet and breathing heavily. O'Bryan stepped off to the side. He unbuckled his leather belt and ripped it out of the belt loops. He held onto the buckle like a knuckle duster and wrapped the belt once around his hand. Maqsood smirked and came in for his attack, but O'Bryan was quick and flicked the tip of the belt into the man's face like a wet towel in a men's locker room full of high jinks. The leather cracked in Maqsood's face and he yelped and recoiled. O'Bryan advanced and flicked twice more, catching the man both times in the face. Maqsood shook his head and lunged with the blade in his left hand. O'Bryan kept his eyes on both blades and swung the belt around Maqsood's left hand. He kicked out and caught Maqsood in the kneecap. Maqsood swung the other blade like a great pendulum and O'Bryan stepped back. He could hear the swish of the blade through the air. He was no longer aware of ambient noise around him, of the screams, the sobbing, the sirens or anything else. For now, it was this moment and nothing else. The belt had become tangled with the blade and O'Bryan whipped it to one side. The knife clattered onto the pavement and slid into the road, but it had slashed the belt and snagged, and the belt shot out of O'Bryan's hand. Maqsood said nothing, but he had noticed that his quarry was now unarmed. He lunged forwards and O'Bryan kicked the blade aside. He looked at the group of terrified children behind Maqsood. There was six or seven-feet between them. More than enough room to duck out from behind the buttress.

"Run!" he shouted. "Now!"

They did, or most of them did, and Maqsood turned around. O'Bryan charged forwards, just two-feet away when Maqsood turned and swung back with the knife. O'Bryan felt the blade go in. He caught hold of Maqsood's wrist and the Pakistani tried to wrench the knife back, but was no match for O'Bryan's strength.

Strangely, it did not hurt. But O'Bryan felt the unnatural presence of the blade, his body aware that it should not have been there. He felt his heart rate go crazily fast, his heart pounding and the blood surging through his veins and arteries. His brain seemed to send out signals too. He knew he had been stabbed, but the brain was reminding him of it constantly. He could feel nausea washing through him. Knew he did not have much time.

O'Bryan could see his daughter. Memories of happy events, snapshots of pictures he had taken. A time before the drink had driven his family away. A time he had wasted and squandered and in his last moments on this earth, a time he regretted losing. He glanced at the two terrified girls from the group; still huddled against the buttress. He was no longer thinking. He was well past that stage now. It was a series of subconscious reasoning – action and reaction. Like knocking a cup from the draining board and putting your toe out to break its fall. You never thought to do it, it was merely reactionary instinct.

All that he could process, was that if he died now, if he dropped and fell, those girls would be Maqsood's next victims. He was already pushing Maqsood backwards. Backwards towards the railings of the viewing point cut into the walls of the bridge. He mustered more strength, more momentum. He kept Maqsood's wrist clamped tight, the blade sheathed within his own body, and powered down through his core, through his strong legs for the final push and slammed Maqsood's back into the iron railings.

3

"I don't get it," Sarah snapped indignantly.

"I'm sorry," O'Bryan said, replacing the binoculars to the top of the bookcase. He closed the glass doors and drew the curtains. He nodded towards the light switch. "It's okay, turn the lights on now."

"Turn them on yourself," she said, walking out of the room. O'Bryan noticed her bare shoulders, the low-cut dress showing them off, along with a tiny dolphin tattoo. It added an air of mystery to her. He wondered if there were any more and where they might be. She flicked on the kitchen light and dropped the bags of take-out on the table, next to a four-pack of Heineken and a bottle of chardonnay. She had everything planned. In the light of the kitchen the low-cut dress looked like part of the plan as well.

"Look, I just…"

"Don't think you can snap at me like that, Ross. I've put up with enough shit in my life, I'm not making the same mistakes again." She placed her hands on her hips, cocked her head and stared at him. "What the hell were you looking at out there anyway? It's almost dark outside."

"I was watching a boat."

"A boat?" She looked at him like he was crazy.

"In the bloody dark, this far up the creek?"

"Yes."

"Probably poachers. You 'seen the deer over there?" her accent slipped a little towards the Cornish end of the scale. "There's stock fencing and a gated entrance to the estate. Much easier to drag a deer carcass down through the woods and into a boat."

"That goes on?"

She shrugged. "It all goes on down here." Her eyes flared for a moment. "No reason to shout at me like you did... I've put up with enough shit, I'll not put up with any more."

"Okay," he said quietly, not sure what she had meant, but certain he would be told in time. He stepped closer and placed a hand on both of her shoulders. It was the first time he had touched her. Her skin was soft and smooth. "It was nice of you to come round."

"You invited me!"

"I did?"

"Yes. The other night. You said it would be nice to just get a takeaway, have a quiet night in."

O'Bryan cursed inwardly. He had said that was what he planned to do, rather than going to The Smuggler's Rest again, where he had taken most of his meals since arriving. Sarah worked there as a part-time barmaid. He had enjoyed her company, enough to go on the date in Truro. However, when she floated the idea of getting together again, he realised that he couldn't miss the second scheduled time and date that Commander Anderson had made for him. He noted, for the thousandth time, that he really was shit socially. Or maybe he was just out of practice.

He looked at her, all red hair and fire in her eyes. She was attractive, but damaged. He could tell that much. But he could tell as much when he looked in the mirror. She was keen on him, that much was true. And women hadn't been beating down his door for the past couple of years. Not since his divorce. Not even before. He studied her eyes. Hazel, glossy. She had an honest face. He could tell being in her company wouldn't be an easy ride. But where was the fun in that? She looked back at him, her expression a little softer now. There was a comfortable height advantage on his part, and she tilted her head upwards. Her lips were soft and pouted a little. He took it as a sign, and leaned in to kiss her. She kissed him back and he relaxed, it wasn't often he read the signs right, but he was about due. She kissed softly, and he matched her. He'd learned early on to step up the pace or tone it down, but whatever you did, match her mood and take your cues. He'd also learned that if you didn't rush this part, you got far more of her later on.

She pulled away and smiled, her expression was one of contentment. "Now that's more like it," she said. O'Bryan leaned in again, but managed to kiss fresh air as she turned around and opened one of the take-out bags on the table. "I got you ribs. Men like ribs. Or you can share my sweet and sour king prawns, whatever, I'm easy…" She turned around. "Well, not easy! I mean…"

O'Bryan regained some composure, managed to put his lips and tongue away in time. "Ribs will be great!" he said, a little too enthusiastically. He was ebbing, the blood pounding through him a little less. So much for his tried and tested strategies.

"I got noodles and rice as well," Sarah said and she went off in search of plates and cutlery. O'Bryan wished her luck, he hadn't used them yet, didn't know where to find them. She bent down and opened a cupboard door. Her backside was shapely in the snug-fitting dress. She seemed to realise this, and dropped down, squatting somewhat elegantly on her heels. She came back up with two plates and put them down beside the food. She smiled at him, a little coyly. O'Bryan couldn't tell if it was an act or a ploy, but he knew he hadn't wanted anybody more in years. She was good, because she all but had him in her hand. "And wantons."

"Great," he said dumbly.

He thought he'd better be pro-active and set about in search of cutlery. He'd found the coffee mugs and he had learned how to use the espresso machine. It probably cost more than his car, which admittedly had seen better days, but still. He drank his coffee black and unsweetened, so hadn't bothered finding a spoon. He never ate breakfast, often skipped lunch and The Smuggler's Rest had provided him with steaks almost as large as the plate they were served on for most of the week. He found the correct drawer and took out two spoons and two forks. Sarah took a spoon from him and set about spooning out the food. She was taking control more than O'Bryan liked, but he hadn't kissed like that in a long time, and if he thought about it, the kiss had been about the best he'd ever had. Sarah's lips were soft and wet and her tongue had been so soft and gentle, probing tentatively. There was a freshness and tenderness he couldn't remember feeling before. One kiss and he was falling hard.

Sarah smiled over her shoulder as she led the way into the lounge. "Got any music?" she asked, coiling herself up on the sofa like a cat.

O'Bryan didn't know. He doubted Anderson's taste in music, or his wife's for that matter, would appeal to the thirty-year-old in front of him. "I'm not sure," he said. In truth, he was hungry now and just wanted to eat.

She shrugged. "So how come you're staying here?"

The question had come as he had bitten into the rib. He chewed, felt sauce on the corner of his mouth. She smiled and leaned forward, wiped the sauce from his cheek with the tip of her finger. She tasted it, then popped a king prawn into her mouth.

O'Bryan didn't know if he was more turned on, or whether it turned his stomach. A little of both, perhaps.

"It's my boss's home. Or second home," he said. "He's from money and so is his wife, so I think he has homes all over the place."

"So why are you here?"

"I'm divorced. I live in a little apartment near Camden Lock. My boss thought I'd do better down here," he said. "For my recovery."

"Recovery?"

"I was injured. Stabbed."

"Oh god!" she exclaimed. "Seriously?"

"Yes."

"No," she sighed. "I meant, were you seriously stabbed?"

"I suppose so," O'Bryan replied. "It's hard to imagine a stabbing that isn't serious."

"Where?" she asked, licking sweet and sour sauce from her lips.

"In London…"

"Oh for god's sake!" she laughed. "I meant, where on your body?" She shook her head and smiled.

O'Bryan smiled too. He hadn't meant to take her questions so literally, but it was funny now. "In my stomach," he replied. "And a gash on my shoulder. It was pretty bad, needed a bit of work inside my stomach to get it all stitched back together."

"Can I see it?"

The question came out of the blue, he hadn't expected it. He hadn't shown anybody else either. Only the medical staff, his own doctor for follow-up appointments and his police federation representative. There was a compensation case in process. He doubted he'd be living in his tiny apartment for much longer. He had been told to get the best deal, he should take six-months leave on grounds of mental anguish. He couldn't have begun to contemplate that. He was champing at the bit to get back to work as it was. And he wasn't one to play the system, or screw it all together. Procedures and human rights, yes. Fake depression, no. In truth he felt pretty good. The wound no longer hurt now that the external stitches and staples had been removed. The internal ones would dissolve soon, if they hadn't already and the wound to his shoulder had been relatively quick to heal. Considering what happened, there were plenty who encouraged him to remain on sick leave, but he had had enough of it already. If it wasn't for Anderson's assignment on the side, he would have asked to go back to work last week.

"I was hoping you'd see it, but not like this," he grinned wolfishly.

"No way!" she laughed. "I'm not sleeping with you if it's all gross and stuff!"

He laughed, but wasn't entirely sure how serious she had been. He put his plate down on the coffee table and wriggled forward to the edge of the sofa. He lifted his shirt to his rib cage. Sarah took in his toned stomach, the remains of his six-pack, which had started to fade after so much time away from the gym located in the basement of his headquarters. He wasn't a serious gym goer, but he tended to go after his shifts, when others headed to the pub. It was easier to be out of the way of temptation, than to skirt the dangers of its periphery, and easier to have a credible excuse. Sarah cocked her head when she saw the scar. It was jagged and approximately six inches long. She reached out slowly and touched it. Her fingernails were sharp, and he flinched a little. She removed her finger, kissed the tip and patted the scar again.

"That will pass. I won't kick you out of bed for that," she said. She leaned in and kissed him again. Softly, her lips open enough to be sensual, but closed enough to signal it was merely a kiss. She sat back in the sofa, tucked her legs underneath herself and picked up her plate. "Did it hurt?" she asked.

O'Bryan picked up a rib and felt the fires below extinguish once more. He bit off a good mouthful and chewed. He'd almost finished it when he said, "At the time, no. I mean, I knew I'd been stabbed, but it didn't hurt. I felt it slowing me down, the effects of the injury. It stung later, and then hurt like hell until I got into the hospital." He realised he did not have a drink. Nor did Sarah. "Do you want a drink?"

"Please."

"Wine?"

"Yes, please."

He got up and walked out to the kitchen, noticing a light that shone briefly past the window. He looked out through his own reflection in the glass, to the quiet road at the rear, or technically, the front of the house. There was a gravelled parking area, enough for three cars, where O'Bryan had parked his old Alfa Romeo. The road beyond connected most of Barlooe, but at this time of night there would only be the odd dog walker or car coming home. The light had looked like a torch. The glow of an orange street lamp lit up a good proportion of the area. There was nobody out there now. He turned back to the table and unscrewed the wine. He's never been a wine drinker, had no issues pouring it into the glass he had taken out of an open display rack. He filled himself a large glass of water and returned to the lounge. He froze, the two glasses in his hands, the wine and water spilling out and onto the oak floor as he stopped abruptly in his tracks.

"Stand still," one of the men said. He was the man with the shotgun, so O'Bryan did as he was told.

The other man was standing behind Sarah, who was still holding her plate. He bent down and knocked it out of her hand, scattering rice, noodles and sauce all over the coffee table. She flinched and let out a little yelp. She was recoiling, almost hugging herself tightly.

Both men wore balaclavas and were both dressed in greasy jeans and work jackets. O'Bryan noted the tattoos on the hands and wrists of the man brandishing the shotgun. He feared shotguns, had seen what one could do to an unfortunate security guard early on in his career. What he feared most was the lack of skill it took to use one with devastating effect. O'Bryan felt dumb holding the drinks. He felt like downing the wine, even though he hated the taste of it.

Fifty-nine days…

"Put down those bloody glasses and kneel on the floor," the man with the shotgun said.

O'Bryan weighed his odds. To someone holding a shotgun he was no threat at all. If they were going to kill him, then they would probably have done it by now. He watched Sarah's expression, but it was one of sheer terror. "Do it!" the man barked. His Cornish accent was thick and he raised the last word of each sentence at least an octave.

O'Bryan stepped across to the dresser and put the two glasses down. He turned around and kneeled slowly. The man behind Sarah stepped around the sofa and O'Bryan could see he held a roll of duct tape. His heart raced, but the barrels of the side-by-side shotgun were menacing and unwavering. The unarmed man was soon behind O'Bryan and he grabbed his arms roughly. O'Bryan did not make it easy for him, keeping his arms locked. The man struggled, but was strong and he pulled backwards against the joints and O'Bryan gave. He wrapped the tape tightly, round his wrists several times. Then he ripped the tape and stood back, pleased with his handiwork. He kicked O'Bryan in the face and he recoiled backwards into the dresser. The man kicked again and again. O'Bryan heard Sarah scream, followed by the man with the shotgun shouting at her to shut up.

"Here, take this," the other man said, holding the shotgun out for his companion. "I want a go." He paced over and the other man took the weapon. He got closer to O'Bryan and swung down a savage punch into his face. O'Bryan felt his teeth crack together. He could feel a chip of tooth somewhere in his mouth. He clenched his teeth tightly as the man rained a series of blows down on him.

O'Bryan's ears were ringing and his eyes were clouded and wet. He was dizzy, and his face felt thick and numb. The other man was laughing. The two had forgotten about Sarah, and she looked as if she was about to move off the sofa when the man now holding the shotgun turned around.

"Where do you think you're off to?" She froze and he walked over to her. He held the shotgun in his

40

right hand grabbed her right breast with his spare hand and gave it a squeeze. "Bugger me, that's got to be nearly three-pound in weight!" She recoiled away and the man laughed. He turned around and shouted to his companion, who was taking a breather from pummelling O'Bryan around the head. "I'm going to give her one, if it's alright with you?" he said. O'Bryan noted that he was better spoken than the tattooed man, little accent and he did not round off his words.

"No!" Sarah shouted.

"Shut up!" the man snapped, spinning around and grabbing her by the wrists. He dragged her off the sofa and she kicked wildly. He pushed her away, then pulled her back with such force that she fell into him. He ducked low and had her over his shoulder with as much well-practised precision as a coalman unloading a fifty-kilo sack. He walked past O'Bryan and handed the shotgun over to the other man and made his way into the kitchen.

O'Bryan tried to stand, but the man kicked him back down, and without his hands to balance or break his fall, he fell into the dresser. The man followed it up with several savage punches, and O'Bryan could feel his consciousness tested. He tried to focus. The man grabbed him by the throat and bent down, staring at him. O'Bryan could see his eyes behind the torn holes in the woollen mask. He noticed the colour of one of the man's eyes had bled into the white. He was reminded of the missing Madeleine McCann's distinctive iris. The man's eyes were dark brown. He drew closer, cigarette smoke on his clothes, a sharp aroma on his breath, enough to make O'Bryan want to gag.

"You hear me?" he said quietly. O'Bryan nodded. He could hardly breathe. He tried to splay his arms, but the bindings were too strong. He nodded again. "Good. Get *yer* arse back in that fancy Italian car and get back to the smoke where *he* belong…" He gave O'Bryan's throat a shake. "You hear *us*?" O'Bryan nodded. The man pushed him down onto the ground. O'Bryan grunted and looked up, just in time to see the sole of the man's work boot coming down towards his face. That was the last he remembered.

4

"And you left the door unlocked?"

"Shouldn't be a crime."

"It's not."

"Then why does it matter?" O'Bryan stared at the man in front of him, glanced across at the young female detective sitting next to him.

"They didn't break in."

"They weren't invited. And they had a gun."

"Just ascertaining the situation."

"Ascertain all you like, but they came in, pointed a gun at us, beat the shit out of me after tying me up and took my friend away saying they were going to rape her."

"You said…" The detective flicked through his notes, "*Give her one*. You never said, rape…"

The female detective looked across at her superior ranking officer. She did not hide the look of contempt. She turned back to O'Bryan, her face impassive.

"Well in the context of taking her by force, and dragging her kicking and screaming, I would say it was safe to assume that *giving her one*, meant rape." O'Bryan sipped the coffee the young female detective had made him earlier and shook his head. "Look, detective…?"

"Detective *Chief* Inspector Trevithick…"

"DCI Trevithick, I'm a police officer myself…"

"I know."

"You do?"

"Of course. This is Cornwall."

"That small, eh?"

"Well connected, that's all."

"My friend…"

"Is safe and well."

"She is?"

"Yes. And she doesn't want to press charges."

"What?" O'Bryan looked at the female detective. "You buy that? Sorry, what is your name?"

"Detective Sergeant Hosking."

"Do you think that is acceptable, DS Hosking?"

"No, it's not."

"Thank you DS Hosking!" DCI Trevithick snapped. He looked back at O'Bryan. "If she doesn't want to press charges…"

"She doesn't have a choice!"

"She might."

"She was abducted! We were threatened at gun point! I was tied and beaten! She can't pick and choose over offences like that," O'Bryan said.

"She's safe and well. She made the call."

O'Bryan alternated the coffee for the tea towel full of ice cubes and pressed the compress against his swollen eye. "Where is she?"

"I said she was safe and well."

"Do you think she knew the attackers?"

"No. Why?"

"Because I can't think of any other reason for not wanting to take this further," O'Bryan said, taking the ice away from his eye socket and cheek. "What happened after she was taken? She called you."

The detective leaned back in the chair. He looked comfortable, unhurried. "Why are you down here?"

"Recuperation, a free holiday," answered O'Bryan. "And *I* asked you a question first. What happened after she was taken?"

"You're familiar with the chain of command, are you not, DI O'Bryan?" Trevithick asked. "I understand you were a DCI once. A long time, and more than a few mistakes ago."

O'Bryan shrugged. "Public record," he said. "Even *you* could look it up."

"Well, I did."

"And what did it say?"

"That you falsified evidence."

DS Hosking looked between the two men. She seemed to be enjoying the cock fight. O'Bryan didn't think she liked her boss much, his comments about rape had shown as much. "What's your biggest case to date, DCI Trevithick? Did it involve cows on the road, or a stolen bicycle? Mine was spending four months of my life undercover with right wing extremists. My last case had me chasing down an Islamic terrorist."

"We *do* get the news down here, DI O'Bryan," he said nonchalantly. "How's the stab wound?" He glanced at DS Hosking. "We have a big city celebrity in our midst. I'm surprised he's not signed up to go into the jungle with all the other celebrities nobody has ever heard of."

"I think they film in the autumn, Sir," DS Hosking said amiably.

Trevithick scowled at her, closed his notebook. "Well, I think we've got all we need."

"Where is Sarah?"

"She's safe. If you don't know where she lives, I certainly won't tell you."

O'Bryan shook his head. "What station do you work out of?"

"Why?"

"So I can call and find what progress you're making."

"I'll get a log number and you can call one-zero-one."

"You may want to re-think that, DCI Trevithick. I'm tired now, but tomorrow is another day. You may want to put your cock away and give me some professional courtesy. You may find your arse bounces off the fucking walls tomorrow and you rethink whether your career is in the Devon and Cornwall Police, or walking around in a yellow high-visibility jacket doing security at the Boardmasters Festival. Tomorrow is the day you may just lose your pension," O'Bryan said, his eyes boring into the man's in front of him. "Now, if you really *have* finished, fuck off out of my house and don't let the door hit your fat arse on your way out."

5

The sun was bright and it shone through the window at the eastern side of the house. The lounge windows faced south, and the sun remained on the house all through the day, with the sun setting over the headland at the highest end of the creek. O'Bryan finally realised why 'south facing' was always a popular phrase touted on property programmes. It really was a feature worth having. He thought about his apartment in Camden Lock. He got the sun for about forty-five minutes a day in the summer months. He couldn't ever recall having seen it from his apartment in the winter. But then, he was hardly ever in. He picked up the post, dropped his head on the pillow most nights for a few hours. His satellite TV had been playing up for a few months now, but he'd never got around to having it fixed. There was little point.

He drank his third cup of black coffee, watched the water subside from the creek. He figured it had been high again at around six-am. It was now eight. The big black and white bird was still dipping for shrimp or whatever it was it was searching for. He looked back at the photocopies of newspaper clippings, the police reports, pathology reports and printouts of internet-based news reports. He had a pattern. And it made him feel uneasy. Singularly, the information was merely a collection of facts and dates. It was the skill of the investigator to create a pattern, use relative assumption and deduct meaning.

The first story was a sad tale, but one told so many times in recent years. The Syrian refugee crisis had become apathetic. So many news features had desensitised the public to their plight. Naturally, there were charities and organisations helping the refugees no end, and the governments of the countries of western Europe had all taken in refugees, some more than others, and given aid to the camps. But it had been news for so long, that it was dropping from the front pages of the papers and the lead features of the programmes, and in some cases, dropped from the schedule altogether. The crisis had peaked with the tragic images of a three-year-old boy. Those images had been the reason Germany had made the short call to allow a million refugees in practically overnight. Alan Kurdi was the little boy whose body was photographed drowned and being removed from the beach near the fashionable Turkish town of Bodrum. It was front page news, and TV news lead story for a week. Celebrities were outraged and talking about nothing else. Some were even going to sing songs. Appeals were made. Slowly, the crisis faded from the news, with one or two pieces a week flashing across the screens of the world. Then Brexit came along and Donald Trump and rockets launched high above North Korea and the world looked inwards for a while, contemplating the insanity on their own doorsteps. War in Syria rolled on, family lines were wiped off the face of the earth. Russia continued to back the Syrian government, the rest of the world complained, but failed to step up and stand up for fear of waking the giant sleeping Russian bear, and refugees continued to migrate to Europe, after outrageous rights such as protection, safety and survival.

Five people changed all of that. For a while, Cornwall had its very own Bodrum. The bodies of the Elmaleh family were found on beaches and rocky sections of coastline from Maenporth to The Manacles, a notoriously dangerous section of reef on The Lizard. Qasim was forty-five-years-old, a doctor and back in his home town of Aleppo, he ran a successful practice, drove a Mercedes and had coached football to under eleven year-old boys. But that was before the war broke out. During the war he had operated on and treated casualties, unpaid, in a city hospital. He moved around a lot, because Syrian government forces and Russian pilots targeted the hospitals. He was an expert in his field as a paediatrician and had studied medicine in both Britain and France. He had even been educated at Oxford for a year on an exchange program. His wife, Yara was also a doctor, who had trained in France. She was thirty-nine, but had taken a career break to bring up their three children. Girls, Amira, aged Twelve and Fatima, aged Eleven and their boy Mohammed, aged ten. She never managed to get her career back on track because of the war, but she assisted her husband in theatre when she could.

It was a tragic story, but one the West was becoming increasingly used to. A family drowned while seeking asylum. The remains of a torn rubber dingy was found on The Manacles. No possessions had been recovered. The bodies had no identification on them, but photo-fits and artist's impressions were made and distributed, largely on social media, and because of Qasim's humanitarian work in Syria, he was soon identified. No arrangements were made to collect the bodies. They had no family in the UK, and no family left alive in Syria. A tragic end to a family who had lived and witnessed more than anybody should. And with the Elmaleh's, an entire family line had ended.

O'Bryan read the reports from a variety of newspapers. The journalism varied in both approach and quality, the local press carried the story on for a while. It was a weekly paper and O'Bryan saw five pieces in all. Nothing new appeared in any of the articles. The last story sparked mentions from the national papers. Cornwall had overwhelmingly voted out of Europe in the referendum, dubbed Brexit. It hadn't done the Duchy much good, the entire county was seen as small-minded and racist, as much of the south of England had voted to remain. The article mentioned the excessive price of Cornish homes, the high percentage of second homes and holiday lets, the lower than average wages and general employment challenges faced by the Cornish. In truth, Brexit was a cry for help with the British government. The Cornish felt marginalised, despite good funding from the EU. O'Bryan read with interest, considering the fact that he sat in the garden of a second home, in a village that was left three-quarters empty during the winter months. The locals in Barlooe worried if their pub would last with such a drop in winter trade. A real problem for villages all over the county. Cornwall had its problems, and all the papers enjoyed a good racist story. Racial hate had come in a form nobody had foreseen.

Good people had stepped up in time and raised both funds and awareness, that this Muslim family would suffer great indignity if they were cremated. Burial was the only method acceptable, and people from the Muslim community came forward with the finances, and arrangements were made for worshipers from a local Mosque to wash and wrap the bodies in an Islamic burial ceremony and a family burial site was secured at the council-run graveyard at Swanvale in the coastal town of Falmouth. It was to most people's horror that the grave was vandalised. Small-minded racially-driven actions by people in a county that had voted out of Europe. Brexit had been hijacked by remain voters who pointed a racist finger at anyone who wanted to change the status quo with

Europe. The people who wanted a halt to immigration, to secure the country's borders had spoken. Cornwall never saw immigration, other than Polish workers who came to pick and harvest what would have ruined in the ground if it had been left to local workers. What Cornwall wanted was recognition from the country's government and a halt to fishing quotas, as well as more freedoms within agriculture. Nevertheless, the county was seen as a last bastion for the small-minded and now the national papers had their racism articles written and published. From a news angle, it could not have gone better.

O'Bryan put down a piece by The Daily Mail. It was as sensational as it had been possible to write. He rubbed his eyes gently. The bruising had come out overnight. He looked a sight. His face was swollen, his right eye puffed shut and he had a split on his top lip. He had chipped a tooth at the back and it felt sharp and rough when he probed it with his tongue. Which was all the time, now that he knew it was there. He drank more coffee, stared out across the ebbing expanse of water. The thought of that poor family, desperate enough to embark on such a dangerous journey, so close at the end. So near, yet so far. They must have been terrified. He looked back at the police and coastguard reports. He made a few notes. He had questions that needed answering. The reports were too light in his opinion. Conveniently so.

6

O'Bryan drove the Alfa Romeo through Barlooe, the burble of the exhaust note echoing off the houses as he briefly travelled parallel with the creek. He wondered if the noise had anything to do with the empty houses. The Creekside houses were large and constructed primarily of glass, chrome and seasoned wood. All hard surfaces and with little in the way of furnishings inside, or open windows to absorb the sound. Like when you viewed an empty house and it echoed in a way that it never did again when you came back and moved your belongings in after renting or buying it.

The road wound round to the left and past The Smuggler's Rest pub. It was just past nine-thirty and a woman was sweeping cigarette butts off the steps and out into the road. The smoking ban hadn't done much for the frontage of places like this. The last time O'Bryan had been in the pub, three-quarters of the clientele had been sheltering from rain in the lee of the porch, as a squall had come up the creek from the sea, leaving O'Bryan alone with Sarah at the bar. That's when they had gelled and he had agreed to her suggestion of a date. It troubled O'Bryan that she had been so forward, in light of what had happened, could it have been merely a coincidence, or had there been an element of gameplay?

He thought about Sarah, needed to know what had happened. Had the men abused her? DCI Trevithick had said that she had not wanted to press charges, but with the events that had transpired, the offences carried out, that wasn't an option. The police would be obligated to investigate and seek criminal prosecution. O'Bryan suspected that Sarah had a complicated past. She had intimated that she had suffered enough, her reaction at him shouting for her to switch off the lights when he had spotted the man looking back at him with the binoculars from across the creek had seemed like a line drawn in the sand. She hadn't been out as much as she had made out, the long-time closure of the nightclub had shown that, and for an attractive thirty-year-old woman, there would have to be a reason for her lack of a social life. Perhaps it was the fact her friends had moved on with partners and had children, or even careers. O'Bryan suspected she had a child herself and was a single mother. Nothing wrong in that. Pretty standard. However, O'Bryan had given thought to the possibility that one of the men had been her lover, or ex-lover and had decided to warn him off with the help of a friend. Small town stuff. In that case, perhaps she had wanted to avoid further problems with an estranged partner, perhaps even her child's father. Maybe she had even reconciled and that was her reason for not wanting to take matters further. He was assuming a hell of a lot, but emotionally, he hadn't been in the best place last night. Sleep had completely evaded him and thoughts always took on another dimension in the early hours.

He slowed the car as he passed the pub. He did not recognise the woman cleaning the steps. He peered through the doorway as he slowed. Should he stop and go in? He thought not. The ex-partner scenario might make more problems for her. He needed to speak with Sarah, but he knew he would need to be discreet. He floored the accelerator and powered past. The road widened and Barlooe was left behind him as he headed towards the A39, the main Truro to Falmouth road.

O'Bryan had done some internet research on his laptop and found what he thought would be the station most likely for DCI Trevithick to be based. Cornwall's policing was a curious affair. Devon and Cornwall Constabulary policed the largest geographical area in the entire United Kingdom. It had to cope with an influx of eleven-million people each summer season, yet the force was shrinking and severe cutbacks had been made. Nothing new there, but the force had closed its principal station in Truro, Cornwall's capital, and another in Falmouth. The constabulary's headquarters were ninety-miles away in Exeter. Many of the stations were faceless facilities where the public could gain no access. A non-emergency telephone number was recommended and a 'we'll come to you' attitude had replaced an approachable policing presence within the community. O'Bryan couldn't see any good from the approach, it served only to alienate people and leave them feeling cut-off from the law. From what he could ascertain, both Bodmin and Camborne stations seemed the only options from where DCI Trevithick and any CID presence could be maintained at any strength.

He chose Camborne as it was closer. The drive took him along a series of sweeping roads. They were narrow, tree-lined or walled in by stone hedges, and extremely fast-moving. Many of the drivers seemed to possess the gift of telepathy, crowning the centre of the road as they negotiated the corners. On several occasions he put the Alfa Romeo's paintwork into the uncut foliage sprouting from the hedges as oncoming vehicles clearly cut onto his side of the road. He was no steady driver, but he felt whisked along in places. He dropped his speed as he entered Lanner. There were digital signs flashing up the thirty-miles-per-hour speed limit, and the drivers at least slowed for these, then raced to the next one in time to hammer on their brakes. This wasn't the Cornwall he had expected. He could see that prosperity found its way into pockets of the county, but this wasn't one of them. There were council houses, new-builds and dilapidated cottages long since extended with block extensions far from keeping them in character. He crowned the hill and drove down into Redruth. He changed his mind about Lanner, but only just. Redruth was an experience, and this coming from a man who had policed some of the most deprived parts of London. He missed the road he needed and ended up skirting around a one-way system to enjoy the sights. There were well-supported shops and buildings turned to flats, but within minutes he was driving through a tree-lined street with grand houses on either side. Huge affairs with gardens and parking. These would have been one or two-million pound homes in parts of London. He doubted they were worth a third of that in this town. They looked old, and O'Bryan remembered reading somewhere that Redruth had been once been a prosperous town, one of the country's leading centres of industry when copper and tin were mined throughout the nineteenth century. A right-hand turn and all this was quickly forgotten and he skirted an area of abject poverty once more. The next couple of miles were taken up with a long road of houses, industrial estates, retail parks, budget foreign supermarkets and a college. Camborne School of Mines seemed in keeping with the mining heritage, this was advertised as a centre of mining and engineering excellence. This stretch of built-up area was Pool and it connected Redruth with Camborne. When he entered Camborne, he changed his mind and re-evaluated Redruth a little more positively. The journey had become progressively more depressing. It was a far cry from Barlooe and the other places like Feock and Mylor he had driven through recently. Cornwall was a county of extremes. There appeared to be a large scale in both income and social divide. He doubted these areas were going to see some of the eleven-million extra people spending their money each summer.

Camborne Police Station was on his left, and he parked easily enough. He followed the signs to the main entrance. The building was constructed from granite with concrete and render extensions. There were traffic police vehicles parked in the lined bays and smaller community policing cars curbing an area of grass. Two uniformed officers exited and walked past him without looking at him. He thought his swollen eye and bruises warranted a second glance, but that was probably one of the reasons why he had made detective at twenty-two.

The man running the desk was a standard-issue community support officer. He was late fifties, growing thickly around his middle and did not look up as O'Bryan entered. O'Bryan coughed. The man continued to tidy some paper and check his computer monitor. He started to type slowly.

"Ross O'Bryan," he said. "I'm here to see DCI Trevithick."

The man did not look up. "He's in a meeting."

"Go fetch him. Tell him to hurry."

The man looked up this time. "Who are you?"

"Today, I'm your boss. Now go fetch him, or your best bet would be to start typing up a new CV."

"Who the hell are you?" The man said, but he had flushed red. His voice was wavering.

"Acting Detective Superintendent Ross O'Bryan, Special Branch," O'Bryan said, then added, "Are you still here?"

The desk officer got up without further word and opened the glass door behind him. He was away from his desk for a few minutes, then came back in and nodded. "He's on his way," he said, his attitude doing a one-eighty. "Can I get you a coffee?"

"No, thanks," O'Bryan said, then turned and looked at the walls. They were mainly of drug-related posters and domestic abuse. There was an anti-terrorism check list, but it was four years old. O'Bryan had helped design the current poster.

Trevithick opened the door and stared at him. "Problem?" he asked incredulously.

"That depends."

"On what?"

"On whether you're in a better frame of mind," O'Bryan said. "Find us an office where we can talk."

"For what?" Trevithick was fuming. "I said all I needed to last night."

O'Bryan reached into his pocket and retrieved two well folded envelopes. He took one and handed it to him. Trevithick pulled out the letter and read. The duty officer was watching from behind the desk. O'Bryan couldn't resist. In ten minutes the whole of the station, and more likely the whole of the Cornish designation of officers would know. "To whom it may concern… After his recent promotion to Detective Chief Inspector, following recent events in the fight against terrorism and subsequent award and commendation for bravery… that was The George Cross, by the way…" O'Bryan added. "The rank of Acting Detective Superintendent has been given to DCI Ross O'Bryan, transcending all of Her Majesty's Police Forces on the United Kingdom mainland and Commonwealth Territories…" O'Bryan smiled as Trevithick lowered the letter. "To surmise, it goes on to say that every courtesy will be extended and co-operation given… signed, the Home Secretary and The Chief Commissioner…"

Trevithick handed back the letter. "What is it you want?"

"Just your undivided time and co-operation. Are we A1 fucking clear on that?"

7

DCI Trevithick led O'Bryan into the CID offices. There were two detectives, both male and late forties drinking coffee by a whiteboard. One was pushing the scales towards overweight a bit too much to run after criminals and the other had had a good go at growing a hipster beard, only it was grey in too many places, at odds with the rest of the ginger, and he had a lot of crumbs in it as well. He held half a Danish pastry in one hand and a cup of something hot in the other. There were photographs pinned to the edges of the whiteboard, a mind-map in the centre. A timeline had been jotted in the bottom right corner. They seemed to be sharing a joke rather than theories.

DS Hosking came out of a side door studying a sheaf of papers. She looked up when she saw O'Bryan and did a double-take. She walked around the row of desks and stood by the two male detectives.

"Is this it?" O'Bryan asked.

"What do you mean?" DCI Trevithick asked somewhat defensively.

"Your CID. Are there more officers?"

"Of course," he nodded. "We have six more out on enquiries into ongoing investigations. There are a dozen detectives stationed at Bodmin, they're all working on cases. And three are on annual leave."

"Who worked on the Elmaleh deaths?"

"The what?"

"The Syrian family who were found drowned near Falmouth."

Trevithick frowned, then nodded. Realisation finally hitting home. "Why?"

"Because I asked you."

"Why are Special Branch concerned with this?" Trevithick scoffed. "And why have they sent down a tainted officer to poke about?"

"Tainted?" O'Bryan felt himself flush. His heart raced. It usually did that before he punched someone in the face. Instead, he said, "Explain yourself, DCI Trevithick."

"You're a DCI, not a regular inspector, I get it. Big deal."

"You read the letter. It's Acting Detective Superintendent, actually."

"Let me see that letter again."

O'Bryan handed him the envelope. Trevithick took it and read it once more. He handed it to DS Hosking. "Get that photocopied, Becky."

O'Bryan swiped it back. She was reading it, her eyebrow raised. "No. Sorry, no copies allowed. Orders." He perched back against a desk. "I need a coffee."

Trevithick cocked a head towards DS Hosking. "See to that, Becky."

She made to move, but O'Bryan caught her arm. He looked back at the two detectives standing by the whiteboard. "Everyone a DS here?"

The overweight man shook his head. "Detective Constable Pengelly, Sir."

"Great. I'll have a black coffee, no sugar, thanks."

DS Hosking smiled at O'Bryan. She turned and placed the sheaf of papers on an empty desk behind her.

DCI Trevithick's face was flushing red with anger. He shrugged and nodded towards his office. "In here, if you please, *Acting* Superintendent O'Bryan."

O'Bryan walked into the office in front of him and moved behind the desk. He pulled out DCI Trevithick's leather swivel chair and sat down, beckoning the man to sit on the plain wooden chair. "I want to talk about the Elmaleh family. I have read the reports, and it would seem that the police report is pretty vague. Downright shoddy, in fact."

Trevithick looked like he was about to implode. He pulled out the chair reserved for his own visitors and sat down heavily. There was a knock on the door and DC Pengelly opened it carrying a cup of coffee. He stared at O'Bryan behind his chief's desk, tried and failed to regain composure, act like it was no big deal, and placed the coffee in front of O'Bryan. He walked back out and closed the door behind him. The office was designed with a large glass wall. O'Bryan remembered when this had become the norm, it made cases of sexual harassment and bullying in the work place as transparent as the window itself. O'Bryan glanced to his right and saw all three detectives and two uniformed officers, who had just dropped in to see the show, looking directly at him. Trevithick side glanced too, he looked back at O'Bryan, thoroughly humiliated. "Vague?" he said, his tone hostile.

"I believe I ended on shoddy," O'Bryan corrected him.

"They drowned whilst illegally entering the country."

"You don't get many illegal immigrants down here," O'Bryan mused.

"What? We're bloody awash with them!"

"Really?"

"Half the workers on the farms are bloody Polish!"

"So legal, then."

"Immigrants!" Trevithick snarled. "Catering, factories, agriculture… You name the job and there's an immigrant in it…"

"DCI Trevithick, you are referring to legal workers from an EU member country," O'Bryan said calmly. He could see the man was boiling. "They're as legal as you and I."

"Not for long! We're heading out of the European Union."

"I'm sure the polish will always be welcome."

"If you say so…"

"So you're not keen on immigrants?"

Trevithick stopped himself. He looked at O'Bryan coldly, but his eyes were dark brown, so he just looked mad. O'Bryan's were grey-blue, and he'd seen enough in life to take the shine out of them. He returned a narrow glare, glacier-cold and unwavering. Unsettling. Trevithick looked away first, as O'Bryan knew he would. "Look, I get it. You're here with a fancy letter and a new promotion, but I've got to work here," he said. "There's nothing amiss with the reports on that family. They came over in a shitty little rubber boat and drowned when it either capsized or ripped."

O'Bryan nodded. "Sad. A whole family, the last of their line, wiped out."

"But the case is closed."

"I'm not happy with the findings."

"*You're* not?"

"Why do you say it like that?"

"Well, you've been sent by someone else. You're staying in Mike Anderson's place at Barlooe. Coincidence? I think not…"

"You know Mike?"

He snorted. "Of sorts. We were at Hendon together. He was fast-tracked before there even was such a programme."

"You were friends?"

"No."

"But you knew him?"

"I *remember* him."

O'Bryan nodded. He couldn't honestly say whether he would have been friends with Anderson, had the man not been his mentor and boss. There was always the barrier of seniority and respect. The man had commanded a lot of respect. Much of what was claimed of his achievements was bullshit. But he had ridden that particular wave and created a legend within the police. The commander of Special Branch, the finger on the pulse of terrorism. The man who ran the department that backed up MI5's intelligence work with hard arrests. It hadn't hurt that towards the end of the Northern Ireland troubles, Anderson had picked up a wounded police officer's weapon and killed an IRA terrorist before he could detonate an IED at a packed tube station. That had secured his status, cleared his path for the top. A legend had been born.

"So you think it was just a case of drowning?"

"Of course!"

"And the vandalism to their grave?"

Trevithick shrugged. "Muslim haters."

"There are other targets. Community centres and mosques. A family's grave is low even for narrow minded racists."

"Then Muslim *immigrant* haters."

"Tell me about the boat."

"The boat?"

O'Bryan sipped the coffee. It can't have been too hot when it was made, so he drank it down in one tepid gulp. It was budget supermarket instant. It didn't hurt to keep the man waiting. He placed the cup down on a letter that was on the desk. There was no signature on it yet, but it had been signed off in Trevithick's name. The cup made a wet ring. O'Bryan lifted it up, placed it down again to make another. He looked up at Trevithick, enjoyed the colour of the man's cheeks. He knew he could be a bastard, and now Trevithick knew it too. "The boat. Tell me about it."

"It was a fucking rubber boat. It ripped or capsized. They drowned. What more do you want?"

"It must have been quite a journey. I'm assuming they came in from France, but it's not the English Channel. This is the mouth of the Atlantic. Hundreds of miles in a rubber row boat?"

"They were desperate."

O'Bryan shrugged. "I'm sure they were. No doubt about it."

"So?"

"So a guy in his mid-forties and a woman knocking forty rowed over from France after walking across Europe from Syria with their three children, all of them under twelve?"

"Perhaps all that walking got them fit?"

O'Bryan stared at him. Trevithick already knew he wouldn't win staring back, so he glanced at his team, who were still looking at the show, and did not even try to busy themselves when he looked at them. "There are two facts here. As sure as day leads to night. One, is that you're a prick. Not a hard, useful prick, but more of a short, thin, flaccid prick of no particular use to anyone. In fact, you're not even a prick. You're a cunt." O'Bryan leaned back in the swivel chair, put his hands behind his head. "The second fact is that the boat did not come over from France. I looked it up. It was a make and model produced in a town called Kuwuwing in the Yunan Provence of China. It wasn't a *bad* boat, a quarter the price of American and European offerings of the same specification, but not the sort of boat you use as a tender to your Four Winds, Bayliner or Regal on the weekends. Not what you want to be seen in at the yacht club. This was the sort of boat a well-meaning dad buys on a whim and comes back to the wrath of his more level-headed wife. It doesn't look as good, but it's a bit of family fun for a week's wages. It can even take a small outboard. I reckon that would be a necessity on a crossing like that. You couldn't hope to row the channel, let alone a crossing all the way to Cornwall. The company made this particular model as a package with an engine, two-piece oars, a fuel tank and four life-jackets. So you can't buy the boat on its own. Other than dads wanting to terrify their families and with their lack of seamanship knowledge, these boats suit cash-strapped fishermen. They don't care what the label on the boat says, or that it looks ten-years-old fresh out of the box…"

"I take it this is going somewhere?"

O'Bryan nodded. "See what happens when you interrupt me again. I dare you," he leaned forwards and placed his hands on the desk, elbowed the ruined letter and a stapler out of the way. He watched Trevithick's eyes for a flicker. It was important to watch now, because if he didn't he wouldn't get his answer. "There was no equipment found along with the Elmaleh family's bodies. No lifejackets, no fuel tank, no oars and no outboard." He reached into his jacket pocket and took out another envelope. He pulled out a series of photographs and dropped them in front of the detective. Trevithick picked them up and studied them one by one. "Although from the photographs you can clearly see from the scuff marks on the plastic transom that an outboard has been attached at some point." He held up a hand to silence the man before he spoke. "Now, I know you're going to say it might have come off and sunk. I mean, the sea here is rough most of the time, isn't it?" He watched Trevithick as the man nodded. "Except that the sea conditions were like a millpond. Not even a shore break. As you well know," he paused. "The second fact, apart from you being a certain derogatory description of a woman's genitalia, is that this boat was never sold in France. Nor was it sold in the rest of Europe. No, after its sale throughout Asia and the US, and its subsequent discontinuation, this boat was only ever sold in Britain as the entire package. I suppose they made the package up, got rid of all the extras they manufactured and moved on to making dildos or toilet brushes or parachutes, or whatever niche they could find and undercut. So, this package makes its way to Britain only. And guess where in particular? No, don't answer that. I dared you after all. You will not interrupt me again. No, this boat was destined to be sold all over the UK, but down here, in darkest Cornwall, one local merchant brought the entire shipment. The boat and package has been discontinued and one supplier, a large independent hardware and maritime depot not three miles from here bought the lot. Now how's that for research?" He leaned forwards and glared at him as he whispered, "That's what we call *detective* work."

DCI Trevithick looked at him, then broke away.

O'Bryan had his answer.

8

"So, you were promoted to super for this assignment?" she asked.

"Acting super, yes," O'Bryan threaded the Alfa Romeo through the traffic and paused as they passed a McDonalds. He was hungry and hesitated a moment before driving on. He was trying to eat well. Five years of drinking and a few falls off the wagon since he had taken his life back and his liver looked like lightly fried Foie Gras. He had been told by his doctor that the damage was entirely reversible. Prior to the incident at Westminster Bridge and his subsequent break in sobriety, he had been hitting the gym and the pool and eating well. He owed himself something better than a Big Mac and a vanilla shake.

"But what is the anti-terrorism angle?" DS Hosking asked.

O'Bryan changed gear, looking at her legs as he drove. She wore a pair of tight jeans, dark and smart. A white figure hugging blouse, her coat draped across her lap. He had requested, or rather demanded she assist him with his inquiries. He needed local knowledge, and he had a feeling she did not like DCI Trevithick after his interview with them last night at the Hemingway House. He thought he might have found an ally. He also thought it may just piss Trevithick off a little more to lose his assistant as well as an entire loss of face.

"There doesn't have to be an angle. My boss was concerned with some details. How he came across this is irrelevant. He was in a position to pull some rank, that's all."

She nodded. O'Bryan glanced at her and she smiled. "So this letter you have, it pretty much gives you carte blanche?"

O'Bryan hesitated before nodding. "Pretty much."

"Well, it certainly rattled the DCI."

"That was my intention. I suppose I went a bit far really. He's just racist, sexist and a bigot underneath, I don't like that. He shouldn't be in the job."

"He speaks highly of you too."

"I suppose he must."

"He said you falsified evidence and the guy got off because of it."

O'Bryan shrugged like it did not matter. But it did. It had become everything, and cost him everything. His rank, his wife and family. The catalyst for so many ruined things, killed-off hopes and dreams. It had been the point to break his sobriety. After two years without alcohol, the failure of the case had left him falling off the wagon and yo-yoing between excess to abstinence. His wife had filed for divorce. He couldn't blame her. He had trouble looking in the mirror sometimes. He owed her some happiness, even if it was his absence that would give her that. "I didn't falsify anything," he said, measuredly.

"Hey, I don't need to know," she said.

"Yes, you do," O'Bryan corrected her. "You're working with me, so I *want* you to know."

"Okay," she said, but he could tell she wasn't particularly bothered.

"We had all the evidence we needed. But there were a few things we couldn't dot and cross, so I left them out. We had more than enough for a successful prosecution and some serious prison time." O'Bryan hit the brakes hard as the car in front misjudged a mini-roundabout. "His defence was a young, hot-shit lawyer making a name for himself. He didn't just pull at the threads of what we, or rather *I*, omitted, he focused on it and virtually nothing else and by the end of the trial he had put so much doubt in the jury's mind, it could only really have gone one way."

"They're good at that," she nodded. "That was a factor of law that I didn't like. Defence lawyers are the worst, I don't know how they sleep at night."

"You and a lawyer traded blows on a case, right?"

She nodded. "He screwed me in the courtroom," she laughed. "He was my boyfriend. I wasn't letting him screw me in *any* room after that," she grinned. "A first class lying bastard. I see the guy he defended sometimes. He's walking around free while his victim is too scared to go out. He's a rapist and my ex knows it."

O'Bryan nodded. "That's why I don't like lawyers." He smiled. "But they're not as bad as your boss."

"No?"

"No. He's a lazy cop. Nothing worse than that. The police are the line between the public and their liberty. When their rights, liberty and welfare are threatened, the police need to do everything in their powers to serve and protect. DCI Trevithick has no love for outsiders or foreigners. Especially immigrants and asylum seekers. His bigotry and xenophobia has cost a family justice."

"He's like a lot of older police down here. They're gradually getting phased out, retired. It's getting better, but there are pockets of the police service where time hasn't caught up. I go to Exeter or Plymouth on a course and it's fine. Just like going back to Hendon for fast track evaluation. Down in some of the places in Cornwall, the smaller towns and communities, and it's lost in the past. Some of the old coppers are dinosaurs. They're guarded and play the game, but after a few drinks and their guard comes down and they loosen up. They're old school. Like they're stuck in the seventies. Sexist, racist and homophobic and would still call a black man a *nig-nog* and a gay man a *poofter* if they had half the chance."

"I take it you're not from around here?"

"No. Hampshire. I moved down here when I finished uni."

"Usually the other way around, isn't it? You live here, go away to university, then have to live away to work off the debts and get a career."

She nodded. "I was lucky, a job came up and I moved. We holidayed here as a family at least twice a year. I sort of felt I grew up here. My father is Cornish and we had his side of the family living down here. Cousins, aunts and my grandad. I had my fondest memories here. I got a job down here with the CPS. I was a lawyer."

"A lawyer!" O'Bryan couldn't help himself. "Sorry," he said, then added, "I'm just not too fond of lawyers."

"Nor am I," she smiled. "To tell you the truth, I wasn't very good. I certainly wasn't a natural. I was dating a lawyer who was super good. And he showed that when he took me apart in the trial. When we split up I just found myself wanting something completely different. I didn't last with the CPS, and couldn't see myself doing property conveyancing and probate for the rest of my working life. I applied for Devon and Cornwall and got in. My law degree got me fast tracked and I made sergeant not long after my probationary period. I like what I do, and I like it more now I'm with CID," she paused. "We're here now. Another fifty-metres on the right."

O'Bryan nodded and turned into the site. It was a compound really, with two units on the one site. He could see access to a massive storage yard gated and fenced between the two buildings. He could see one marked tools and hardware and the other marked as marine goods and clothing. There were plenty of spaces and he parked the Alfa as far away from the other cars as possible. DS Hosking opened her door and got out. O'Bryan glanced at her rear as she pushed herself up. He hadn't intended to, but was pleased he had. She was attractive and had a good figure. She had a comfortable demeanour as well, and he had talked easily with her. He was glad he had chosen her to work with over the overweight detective, or the one with half a Danish pastry in his beard.

They walked in through the automatic doors and DS Hosking hovered around the counter, but O'Bryan walked on past and down one of the cluttered aisles. She looked unsure for a moment, then followed him.

"What are you doing?" she asked, frowning at him.

"I like to get a feel for a place first," he said. "Take it all in a bit." He carried on walking, perusing some of the shelves, then stopped when he entered an area with marine and maritime equipment and clothing. He could see two boats and a small selection of canoes. They were open types and as he drew near, he noticed that these were inflatable models as well. He tapped the hull of one of them, surprised at how sturdy and rigid it was.

"We're here to look at the boat," she chided, nudging past him and standing in front of the yellow inflatable. "Not kayaks."

The boat was fitted with a three-horsepower petrol outboard and slotted into the straps on the sides were a set of oars. Four lifejackets lay in the hull.

"Beauty, isn't she?" a middle aged man wearing a sweatshirt with the store's logo on it said, walking up to them. He banged a fist on the boat and smiled. He didn't have many teeth in his smile, but it hadn't put him off trying. "I bought one of these beauties myself. All this for four-hundred quid. We change the sizes of the lifejackets to fit your crew, they have to fit just right if you have kids going out."

"It looks good," O'Bryan said. He pointed to the fuel tank, which looked like a squashed plastic petrol can, only a little larger. "How many miles can the tank take you."

"It's hours with boats," he smirked. "That will run this engine for about three hours."

"And how fast will it go?" DS Hosking asked.

"About six knots, which is about seven miles per hour, but you have to watch the tides. If you put in at Falmouth and head for some dinner at The Pandora, and the tide's running a four knot drop, then you'll get there in time for tea," he said with a largely toothless grin.

"The Pandora?" O'Bryan frowned, but he realised it must have been a restaurant on the river. He'd been thrown about dinner and tea. He'd never heard it used as a replacement for lunch and dinner before. In London if you booked for dinner you'd get the evening slot and told that tea came in a pot with some cakes.

"It's a pub on the river," DS Hosking said. "The Pandora Inn."

"You two aren't together then?" the man asked.

"We're colleagues," O'Bryan said quickly.

"I see…" the man smirked. He had a vision of what these *colleagues* would be doing in the boat. "Anyway, the boat's a good laugh, but it pays to check the conditions out first and not to overload it. The engine's alright, but what you have to remember is we sell five-horsepower Honda and Mariner outboards for between six and seven hundred pounds. This deal is an absolute bargain."

"Could it take four adults?"

The man shrugged. "We've done it, but it would be best for two or three. Or a couple of adults and a couple of nippers."

"So six knots and a favourable tide, and the boat would get you about twenty-one miles?" O'Bryan queried.

The man thought for a moment, but he was looking directly at DS Hosking's breasts under the close-fitting blouse as he did the sums, so O'Bryan figured it would take a while.

"I suppose," he said eventually. "But if you're running with a good tide, you could get that up to thirty. I wouldn't do it though. I explore the creeks in ours, or go out half a mile and drop a fishing line or two. It's a good boat because of the chambers. Stick a hook in one, and you've got nine more full of air. But like I said, great for dinner at The Pandora, but you'd better know what you're doing there."

"Why is that?" O'Bryan asked.

The man took his eyes off DS Hosking's breasts for long enough to look at her face. "You know that, don't he?" he laughed. "Because thirty people supping wine and pints of Rattler will be wanting you to fail mooring to the pontoon and take a swim with your clothes on! I'd sit there all bloody day if the wife would let me, just to watch a posh prick in his hundred-grand rib smack into the pontoon! You'd be alright in this though. These are cheap as chips and people know it, so aren't bothered with you. I watched someone take ten attempts to moor up once in a Bayliner, then his wife drops down to her fanny in the water, just the one leg mind, she gets it back up before the rest of the boat hits and cracks on the pontoon. We all had a good laugh at that one!"

"Sounds delightful," O'Bryan commented. "So how many of these have you sold?"

"Hundreds."

"Wow. Just from this store?"

"No. We're all online now. We've sold loads on the internet." O'Bryan tried hard to hide his disappointment. The trail was almost impossible, but the internet sales closed the gap from almost to completely. "That's the only one left, so if you want it today, I'll deflate it and pack it up for you and we'll call it three-fifty."

"Thanks for your help," O'Bryan said, turning his back on the man. The man got the message and didn't linger. He walked somewhat dejectedly back down the aisle.

"So?" DS Hosking looked at him. "The internet sales make it difficult."

O'Bryan nodded. "There's CCTV on the doors, but none I can see throughout the store."

"They might have hidden cameras?"

"No point. CCTV is a deterrent. They don't want to catch people, merely stop them stealing. I doubt they get much of that anyway. Most of the stuff here is big and bulky. Perhaps the other shop with packets of screws or tools or lightbulbs, but here it's all rope and buoys and rubber fenders. And the cash registers are literally in the doorway."

DS Hosking nodded. "Okay. So we've ascertained that the boat isn't all that sturdy for four adults, but would probably be alright for two adults and two children. The Elmaleh family were a party of five…"

"But the children were young and small. They had been on the move across Europe for a year. They weren't pushing obesity and eating Happy Meals and playing on an Xbox," O'Bryan interrupted. "But no outboard was found, no fuel tank either, although that tank wouldn't be enough to cross from Calais to Dover, let alone anywhere else."

"Those oars look a bit flimsy as well," she added.

"What else?"

She frowned, walked around the boat, then looked at O'Bryan and shrugged. "The chambers!" she blurted. "It has ten individual chambers, so a rip might not necessarily sink it."

O'Bryan nodded. "What else?" She thought for a moment, then shrugged again. O'Bryan patted the side of the boat. "It's yellow. It's as bright as the sun. If I were in France, knowing that all that stood between my family and a new life in a country I knew and felt we had a future in, was a hundred or two hundred miles of ocean, I would find something more suitable. More substantial. It wouldn't be a budget rubber boat and it most certainly wouldn't be yellow."

She nodded. "Fair point," she said. "But beggars can't be choosers."

"Exactly," O'Bryan said. "And despite war in their country, and despite the terrible humanitarian crisis, I have dug a little further. Done DCI Trevithick's job for him, so to speak. The Elmaleh family were not beggars. Far from it. Qasim Elmaleh withdrew the Syrian pound equivalent to two-hundred and sixty-eight thousand pounds Stirling from various accounts, as the war in Syria took hold and it started to look like it would not be a short-term uprising, like others had been during much of the Arab Spring. He sold off assets for cash as well. The Elmaleh family were extremely middle-class and well educated. They came from money. They had more than I'll ever earn or could dream of putting aside. This entire refugee crisis has dehumanised people, objectified them. Pricks like DCI Trevithick see people as illegal immigrant scum. But what if the tables were turned? What if the British government waged all-out war on its people because we were unhappy with the way they ran things. What if the army, the RAF and the Royal Navy bombed us all? Imagine the SAS going in house to house to kill *dissidents*. Now we can't leave, we can't work, we can't buy food…" He shook his head. "Unthinkable, isn't it?" She looked thoughtful and he could tell she hadn't given it much thought until now. O'Bryan hit the side of the boat with his fist and shook his head. "No. The Elmaleh family did not set out in that boat," O'Bryan said.

"And I don't think they set out on their own from France at all."

10

O'Bryan unfolded a map and spread it out between them in the front seats of the car. He found the approximate area with Falmouth at the bottom left corner. "Go on then, DS Hosking, show me where the Pandora Inn is."

"What has it got to do with the case?"

"Nothing. But I'm bloody starving and haven't eaten since my three bites on a barbecued rib last night."

"I don't know if I should…"

"Oh bloody hell, Hosking! It's a bit of lunch," he said and started the car. "I've got it covered."

"Okay," she relented. "Just lunch?"

"What else?"

"Of course, lunch," she said and opened out the map further. She looked a little flustered, as she ran her finger across the map. "It's here. But we don't need the map, I can direct you."

O'Bryan studied the map for a moment. "So Point Geddon and Barlooe Creek are over the next two headlands?"

"Yes," she said.

"Malforth Manor backs down onto Barlooe Creek."

"So?"

"No reason," he said casually. He folded the map and dropped it into her foot well. "Right. Out of here and right towards Redruth, yes?"

"Yes," she said.

She sat back in her seat and seemed to relax. Her window was open a little and the wind came through and pressed the blouse closer to her skin. If that was possible. O'Bryan glanced at her, but he needed to remain professional. Although he had only recently met her, with the exception of last night's farcical interview with DCI Trevithick, he liked what he saw. DS Becky Hosking was sharp, intelligent and attractive. The full package. He glanced at his face in the rear view mirror. What would she think of him? Ten years older, greying ever-so-slightly at the temples, his eyes lifeless and grey? Arrogant and bullish? Now covered in bruises with a swollen eye. He mentally shrugged it off. He wasn't twenty anymore and he was fine with that. He had felt stagnant and rutted of late, but he'd had two dates this week already and was falling for another woman, so it wasn't all bad. The thought made him question Sarah and her well-being after last night. He had been told that the woman was alright, but he made a note to find her tonight and hear her side of events. Whether it was a past or present lover, whether she could talk more about it, whether he could convince her to be willing to press charges if the two men were ever found. But he wouldn't hold his breath.

Once they left Redruth and then Lanner behind them, the road was clear and swept through wooded areas and small fields and paddocks. It was hilly terrain, and they dipped low in a valley before DS Hosking told him to take a left, a 'shortcut' she knew. The road was narrow and two cars would never pass, but there were a few passing places cut into the tall hedges. They crossed over the busy A39, the main road between Truro and Falmouth, and took a steep hill through woods, which meandered through the countryside passing single, and rather expensive looking houses set back from the road with large gardens and wooded entrances. Hosking had commented about living here when the lottery numbers came up. O'Bryan would have to agree. His DCI wages were not going to cut it here.

The hill down to Restronguet Creek greeted them with a wonderful view across the water to Restronguet Point. The tide was in and the sun glistened upon the surface of the water. Boats were moored in the middle of the river and swans glided peacefully between them.

O'Bryan swung into the carpark and was lucky enough to see a car reversing out of a space. He gave the driver room, then drove in and parked. As he opened the door and got out, he noticed that the car park was full.

"It gets busy here," DS Hosking said, as if reading his thoughts. "Lots of people park and walk down to Mylor. They won't all be eating."

The pub itself was eighteenth century and dark. O'Bryan skimmed his head on the roof and flinched, thankful it had padded cushion fixed in place. He hovered at the bar, DS Hosking catching him up. "Soda water and lime, please," he asked.

The barman looked expectantly at Hosking. "Make that two," she said, then turned to O'Bryan. "I'd have a wine, but on duty and all…"

He nodded in agreement. Duty was always his favourite excuse. Duty and driving. And the gym.

Sixty-days…

The waiting staff bustled through with plates of food. O'Bryan eyed a huge sandwich which looked to be crab. It looked good. He pulled a menu out from a rack in front of the till and opened it up. The drinks were placed on the bar and the barman asked if they wanted anything else. O'Bryan ordered the vast crab sandwich and DS Hosking hurried with her choice, feeling the pressure to pay. Despite needing a table number outside, O'Bryan pointed to a table through the window and paid with cash.

They walked out with their drinks and were about to sit, when a couple moved from a table on the pontoon.

"That'll do," he said.

"You'll play havoc with their ordering system."

"Well, they'll have to use their initiative," he commented flatly and led the way down the steep wooden walkway and onto the pontoon. As he sat down at the picnic style table, he watched a boat slow its revs and steer a course straight for them.

"This is what the bloke at the marine supplies outlet was talking about," DS Hosking said and sipped some of her drink.

O'Bryan watched, as did forty other people. Some put down their cutlery to watch. Another took out their phone and started to film. O'Bryan shook his head. "Voyeuristic bastards," he said, but continued to watch all the same.

The boat slowed and came in on a large arc. The man at the helm was in his late-fifties and the woman O'Bryan assumed to be his wife stood on the prow with a rope at the ready. The boat glided right up to the pontoon and the man throttled back and engaged reverse. The engine changed pitch and the boat stopped dead in the water. The man switched off the engine and the woman threw the rope to a man who had stood up from his table and offered a hand. She stepped off the boat and thanked the man as he wound the rope tightly around a cleat. The man at the helm leapt down and nodded thanks. The onlookers turned back to their drinks and meals and paused conversations, but there was an air of disappointment. Professionalism was not rewarded with this crowd.

"Didn't go as well as that for me and John," DS Hosking said dryly.

"Your ex?"

She smiled. "He has a large boat. Half as big again as that one." She nodded towards the Bayliner. "He was a bit throttle-happy at the best of times. He came in too fast. Shouted at me, but I didn't know what the hell I was doing, didn't know a thing about boats, and I got in a mess with the ropes. He hit the pontoon so hard people's meals ended up on the deck. He smashed the front of the boat in…"

"Prow," O'Bryan smiled. "You're not kidding you know nothing about boats!"

"Shut up!" she laughed. She looked up as a waiter drew near. "That's us!" she called out. "Two crab sandwiches and a bowl of chips… sorry, we moved table…"

The waiter put down the round plastic tray and off-loaded the meals, along with a bucket full of cutlery, napkins and some condiments. When he left they both picked up their doorstop sandwiches and ate quietly.

"So, Sarah Penhaligan…" DS Hosking ventured. "You're an item?"

O'Bryan shook his head, a little too adamantly. "We got chatting at The Smuggler's Rest, the pub in Barlooe. We had a date afterwards in

Truro. She popped round with Chinese food last night. But it was a misunderstanding. She thought I had invited her, but I had said I wanted a quiet night in with a takeaway."

"Jesus. I was just asking, Casanova…" she smiled.

"Well, I…" he stopped. He simply bit into more of the sandwich. If he filled his mouth with food, he wouldn't make more of an idiot of himself. He underestimated the amount of crème fraiche and a good dollop went onto his shirt. He scraped the excess with the clean blade of his unused knife and tutted loudly. "Sorry about that…"

DS Hosking dipped the edge of her paper napkin into her lime and soda and reached over and dabbed at it. She looked up at him and then said, "Sorry, I don't know why I did that…" She looked away, sipped some of her drink.

"Thanks," he said light heartedly. "I'm such a boy sometimes, women just end up mothering me…"

"Sarah Penhaligan," she said. "Did she try to mother you?"

O'Bryan shook his head. "I don't think so. Do you know her?"

"Why?"

"You seem to have an opinion on her."

"I do?"

He shrugged. "Just sounded like that."

"Sorry, unprofessional."

"You're not a doctor, you're a copper," he said. "If you have an opinion, get it out there."

"No, I…"

"Spit it out. Shit, one date and a misunderstanding. Two kisses."

"There were kisses?"

"I'm irresistible, what can I say?" he smiled.

"I knew her from holidaying down here. She's the same age, give or take."

"And she got about? Shit, I'm divorced with a child I don't see. We all have a past."

"You have a child?"

"Yes. Is that a problem for you?"

"No. Why would it be?"

"Because you're acting like you're interested, and it's only been a morning, but I'm as interested in you as it's possible to be," he said, glancing at his watch. "After three hours and twenty-seven minutes…"

She laughed. "Well, we could see how this pans out and take it from there."

"Sounds like a plan." He smiled. "Of course, if you feel pressured by a senior officer, feel free to call your federation rep."

"I'll be okay," she said, then chuckled. "Well, you can make your own judgements on *Ms* Penhaligan."

"Perhaps," he said non-committedly. "But I want to find her and see if she knows anything about last night, or if she's okay, despite DCI Trevithick's word on the matter."

"Well, I might know where to find her," she said.

11

The road from Mylor towards Point Geddon, like much of the area, was lined with trees and interspersed by paddocks and fields. The hedges were high and covered with foliage, and for much of the route, the trees topping the hedges grew over the road in arches, their branches meeting and forming a tunnel of thick green leaves. The sun shone through the canopy, occasionally blinding O'Bryan in its glare when the foliage thinned. He wished he'd brought some sunglasses with him. He looked across at DS Hosking, who with her dark, glossy hair, dark Gucci sunglasses and tight-fitting white blouse, looked like chic personified. She swept a lock of hair away from her face, the breeze blowing through her half-open window.

O'Bryan slowed as they approached a grand entrance on their right. The signage was carved elegantly into a slab of granite at least six-feet square. He downshifted the Alfa Romeo and slowed to a crawl. Beside the sign was a colourful banner promoting an event for a local charity tomorrow night. It advertised champagne and free bar, an auction, canapés and a house tour. The main event was a raffle draw for a car supplied by a local BMW and Mini dealership. There was a number to call and a weird black and white symbol in a box.

"Malforth Manor," she said.

"Their land backs down all the way to Barlooe Creek?"

"That's right," she nodded. "Why are you interested?"

"Just something I need to check," he replied. "Later." He took out his phone and took a couple of pictures of the sign.

"Just scan the QR box," DS Hosking said. "It will take you right to their website."

He looked at her, then to his iPhone. "I wondered what those things were."

"You're kidding, right?" She laughed. "They're all over London." She snatched the phone out of his hand and flicked through the screens. Then she opened an app and held it up to the sign. "That's it," she said, then looked at the phone, disappointed. "Can't help the Cornish phone signal though. You've got no bars."

"I barely have since I've been here."

"Well, when you get enough for internet access, go to this app…" She showed him and passed the phone back to him. "It will tell you all about the event being held at Malforth Manor. Either that, or the charity Ogilvy is raising money for."

"Ogilvy?"

"Charles Ogilvy is the Lord of the Manor, or likes to think he is. He's not really a lord, or *any* type of nobility, but he acts like it. He came from money, but made a load more on his own. Filthy rich. He owns other properties, mainly holiday homes. He's responsible for keeping the Cornish out of homes and driving them to where property is more affordable, according to some."

"And is he?"

"Doubtful," she scoffed. "He owns some of the most luxurious homes down here. They aren't the sort of properties to keep low earners or key workers off the property ownership ladder. But his properties still manage to piss people off. They are usually big and modern looking, stay empty for half the year, so that kills local trade and communities."

O'Bryan nodded. "There's quite a few of those in Point Geddon and Barlooe. I thought they would be rented up until October half term at least."

"I think the seasons are getting shorter. Parents can't take their kids out of school either side of the holidays. Businesses are suffering for sure. I think affordable cottages do okay, but some of those houses on the creek rent out for seven grand a week."

"What?" O'Bryan shook his head. "Well, they should all make their investment money back soon," he said. "So Ogilvy makes that kind of money?"

"All day long. He owns care homes across the county as well. There was some controversy a few years ago. He does, or at least *did*, deals with the people going into his homes, along the lines of buying their houses and releasing the equity which he would then off-set against their care fees."

"And the families objected?"

"Exactly. He made his accounts available and it showed good value in terms of ancillary care, but the houses were woefully undervalued and he paid far less than market rate. He was the silent partner in a letting and estate agency. The properties ended up being let out or sold through the agency, but they came into the company at a far higher investment price than the old people were given. Ogilvy couldn't account for the deficit and ended up paying a fortune in personal taxes. It was all over the local papers, but he's done a lot of charity work since and everyone loves him again." They entered Point Geddon and DS Hosking pointed left towards the river. "Down that road," she said. "See the big house on the quay?"

"Yes."

"That's it."

"Really?"

"Really," she said. "I'll wait in the car. Don't get *too* reacquainted."

He smiled and parked up behind a ten-year-old convertible Mini Cooper. He got out and shut the door without saying anything. In truth, he was a little embarrassed. He hadn't thrown himself into anything before the date with Sarah. And he had felt comfortable kissing her last night. But something did not feel right, and that only came about when he had spent time with Becky Hosking. He had never had relationships with colleagues, but this time he seemed to be able to justify it somehow. He had only known her for a matter of hours, but he felt something he had never felt before. Not even with his wife, the woman he had vowed to be with forever. He thought of spending more time with DS Hosking. The idea appealed to him. And it wasn't just the fact that it would be driving DCI Trevithick crazy.

There were an open set of wrought iron gates, painted black with gold paint on the spear-tips. It looked a little too Cheshire for O'Bryan. For the rest of the village too. There was a 'for rent' sign attached to the railings by a company called Clive & Gowndry. The gravel on the drive was grey slate chips, both large and thickly applied. The borders were weeded and heavily planted out with flowers and plants and the earth was covered with bark chips. It looked as if a gardener had worked hard on the beds over the summer. O'Bryan stood and looked at the house. It was large and square, and constructed from granite, the cement new and repointed. The roof looked new also and the windows were triple-glazed and from the discreet tubing above, looked to be self-cleaning. Sarah Penhaligan worked part-time shifts at a local pub. There was no way she would afford this, and even if she could, through inheritance or windfall or even hard work, a few hours at minimum wage wasn't going to make a bit of difference.

He rang the doorbell and stood back. He could see a figure moving behind the quarter section of smoked glass in the dark oak door. It looked like Sarah, and she seemed to stop and look at the wall before opening the door. O'Bryan realised it had been a mirror. He stood back a step and smiled. "Glad to see you're…" he paused. She was wearing a figure-hugging leather dress that would have been an effort to get into, and it was so short that it barely covered her knickers. "…okay," he said.

She looked visibly shocked when she saw him. She managed to regain some composure, but frowned and looked past him warily. "Ross?" she said. "What are you doing here?"

O'Bryan recovered quickly, or thought he had. His face still questioned her appearance. "Sorry, I wanted to see if you were alright, after last night."

Again she looked past him. "Fine, just a misunderstanding, that's all."

O'Bryan smiled, but his expression dropped almost as quickly. He walked in, barging her out of the way. She over-reacted, feigning an act of losing her balance and looking surprised. He wasn't having any of it. "Bullshit!" he snapped. "Shut the fucking door and listen to me…"

She did as he ordered, stood back from the door and smoothed the dress over her hips. It was a challenge to breath and keep her intimate area covered. "I..."

"Shut up!" O'Bryan glared. "Last night, two men threatened me with a shotgun and tied me up.

They beat the living crap out of me, and the last I saw, you were being manhandled out of the house with the threat of a man taking you for sex, *apparently* against your will. You don't get to pick and choose. I want to know who they were, and you have to make a statement. Which you can do tomorrow morning at nine o'clock, to me in person, at Camborne police station."

"But…"

"I said, shut up!" he snapped again. "DCI Trevithick. You know him, right?"

"Yes."

"What happened when the guy took you away?"

She shrugged. "Nothing."

"He said he was going to *give you one*," O'Bryan said. "You were kicking and screaming, that would suggest he was going to rape you."

She shook her head. "No."

"So he didn't rape you or sexually assault you?"

"No."

"What then?"

"He said he was there to warn you off. That I should go and forget all about it."

"And that was that? He let you go?"

"He did."

"Well, thanks for your concern," he said coldly. "You didn't think to see if I was okay?"

"I called the cops!"

"And said what?"

"That there'd been a fight."

"A fight? It was more than a fight, Sarah. They had a gun, they tied me up…"

"Look, I called the police, but I don't want to get involved."

"Did you know the men?" She hesitated. O'Bryan watched her closely. "Well, did you?"

"No."

O'Bryan turned and walked out of the hallway and into a spacious lounge. It looked out on the creek, just a mile closer to the sea than the Hemingway House. "This is a million-pound view," he said. "How are you here?"

"Thanks!"

"You're a barmaid," he retorted. "You work part-time."

"It belongs to a friend," she conceded quietly, solemnly. "He's letting me stay while I get straight."

"Where are your things?"

"What?"

"There's nothing *in* here," O'Bryan walked out into the kitchen. She followed, tottering on her high heels. He looked around the kitchen, opened the fridge. "Nothing. Not even milk. The fridge isn't even switched on."

"Get out!" she snapped venomously. Then added, "How did you know I was here? Who told you?"

"A colleague."

"That bitch Becky Hosking," she laughed. "I thought so. DS *Bloody* Hosking."

"You've got history then?"

"And then some," she seethed. "She needs to let it go."

"What?"

"Ask her," she said. "I'm done talking. I'll make that statement tomorrow, until then…" She walked back out to the hallway and stood by the door, her hand resting on the door handle. She waited for O'Bryan to catch up. "Goodbye then…"

He looked at her incredulously. "DCI Trevithick told you not to get involved, not to make a statement, didn't he? Why?"

"Ask him yourself. I'm done."

"He knows you're a prostitute?"

She glared at him, but he could see the sadness in her eyes, and there were tears forming making them glossy and vulnerable. "Just go, please…" she said quietly. "I thought I saw a way out of all this with someone like you. Someone who didn't know what I have had to do, someone who took me for what they saw and liked me… And now you're standing there, *judging* me. Well life isn't always a bed of roses and you don't get to know people's pasts or secrets, or what they've had to do."

"Sarah…"

"Just go!" she snapped and turned around, facing the door. She was crying. She cupped her face and the skirt was so short it rose up to reveal a flash of red silk underneath. O'Bryan put a hand on her shoulder and she flinched away. "Stop it, leave me alone," she said sadly.

O'Bryan opened the door and stepped out. The door slammed behind him and he felt the wind off it against his back. He stepped down onto the gravel and walked back to the car without looking back. As he reached the car, a man in his fifties slinked around the hedge and railings and walked across the gravel driveway. He was overweight and balding. He fidgeted nervously on the doorstep. He rapped on the door and stood back. O'Bryan watched as the door opened, Sarah out of sight behind it, and the man stepped inside. The door closed and O'Bryan got back into the car.

"You're welcome," DS Hosking said.

"What for?"

"You swerved a messy situation with that one. Good job it ended at a Chinese takeaway and a kiss."

"She doesn't like you much," he commented.

"She said that? I'm hurt," she smirked.

"How do you know each other?"

"I'm a police officer. She's a whore. Our paths have crossed."

"She said you should just *let it go*. What's that about?"

"No idea. She doesn't like being nicked, that's all."

"Are you going to nick her now?" O'Bryan asked. "That guy could do with a shake down."

"Oh, he's *getting* that for sure."

"I meant arrested. I'll bet he's married with kids. What makes someone risk all of that?"

"Sex."

"Figures," O'Bryan shrugged. "I hope it's worth it. Losing a family makes you rethink just about everything in your life."

"And that happened to you?"

O'Bryan started to the car and reversed back out onto the road. He said nothing, but he felt there was much to ask. He just needed to get the questions in the right order.

12

"So what are we doing at your house?" DS Hosking laughed. "It's a bit too soon for me. I just meant we'd have a drink when we've finished your investigation, see where it goes."

O'Bryan looked at her and smiled. "I want to check something out."

"I bet you do."

"Come on, you'll see," he said. "How are you with boats?"

"I told you, I don't know what I'm doing and don't know which end of the rope to hold."

"Well it's not a thirty-foot power boat, and this isn't the Pandora Inn," he said and opened his door.

DS Hosking followed. They walked around the side of the house and out onto the lawn. The tide was still coming in and three swans glided in with it. The sun was high above them casting a hue of gold across the water. "This is gorgeous," she said.

"Pretty idyllic, isn't it?" He looked out across the water. "I don't miss London when I stand out here and look at this."

"You could put in for a transfer," she quipped. "Look at it every day."

He smiled. "It's not my house, remember? I got cleaned out during my divorce. Unless I get some compensation for my injury, I'd be in a two-bed new-build semi on an estate someplace, wouldn't see a view anything like this in the morning…"

She chuckled. "Well, a view is always free. Just take an interesting route to work. So what boat is it, and what the hell are we doing?"

O'Bryan stopped and looked at the upturned boat. He wasn't sure what it was, but he went with a big rowing boat. He pointed at the hull. "That."

"That?"

"Yes."

"I've never rowed."

"Good. That makes two of us," he said. "But it can't be that difficult."

"Famous last words…"

They caught hold of each end of the boat and turned it over. It was heavy and cumbersome, but once it tilted so far, it spun freely and slipped out of their hands, the hull dropping heavily onto the area of chippings that had been laid aside for the boat and the remains of two broken-looking canoes. The quay was a three-foot drop to the shingle and mud beach, but at high tide O'Bryan had noticed it was over two-feet deep with water. They lowered the boat down onto the beach and O'Bryan jumped down, instantly sinking to his ankles in the mud. He pulled a face and DS Hosking laughed. She kicked off her leather boots and rolled her tight jeans over her calves.

"That mud stinks now that you've broken it up!"

She was right. O'Bryan screwed his face up at the stench of rotted fish and vegetation and dragged the boat into the water. DS Hosking picked up the oars and handed one to him. O'Bryan got into the boat first, his muddy shoes streaking the fowl-smelling mud over the cream-coloured hull. He positioned himself on the forward bench and steadied the vessel with a hand on both sides. It did nothing to right the tilt of the boat as DS Hosking got in and slipped down onto the rear bench. She fumbled with her oar and the boat drifted out into the river.

"Here, give me the other oar," he said.

He got both into the rowlocks and started to row. It didn't go well and for the first five minutes the boat went in every direction but where he wanted it to go, and he caught the occasional oar on either the muddy bottom, or just got it wrong and the oar slipped out of the rowlocks and left them spinning in circles.

"Can I have a go?"

"You think you can do better?"

"I think it would be impossible to do any worse…"

He pulled the oars back in and set about transferring his weight across to the rear seat as she did the same. Unsurprisingly, this was difficult as well and the boat almost capsized when his three and a half stone premium on her weight almost sent him over the side. Now in each other's seats, DS Hosking set about placing the oars in the rowlocks while O'Bryan clutched onto both sides. To his annoyance, she skulled the boat around and rowed in a fairly straight line towards the far bank.

"The world and his dog hates a show off," he said.

She smiled. The sun lit up her face. He noticed her eyes were as blue as the sky and her hair was darker than pitch. She had a slight tan, which brought out her eyes. She was quite possibly one of the most beautiful woman he had ever seen. And she seemed more so the longer he was in her company. "I take it we're heading for the jetty?"

"We are."

"Makes sense. I wasn't sure where you were going."

"I was just familiarising myself with the river," he said. "Getting an idea what the tide was doing." He grinned. She rowed well, her breasts straining against the material of the blouse. Her arms looked toned and he could tell that her stomach and core were strong. "You've done this before, DS Hosking."

"Do you still want to ask me out for a drink when we're done?"

"I might. It's only been a day."

"Well, call me Becky," she said. "Can you do that, *Superintendent*?"

"*Acting* Superintendent."

"I have a feeling you'll be DCI very soon."

"Why?" He looked shocked.

"I don't think you make things ride easily for you."

"No?"

"No."

He shrugged. "Easy come, easy go."

The jetty loomed and she took the oars out of the water. The boat glided slowly towards it, then nudged the timber edge. "It's deep here," she said. "Look. The bottom is six-feet deep, I'd say."

"The bank is sheer. That's how they got a bigger boat in here last night."

"Who did?"

"I saw a boat come in at dusk. You see that tree?" He pointed at the submerged tree and she nodded. "That hid the boat from view."

"What kind of boat?"

"A fishing boat. On old and battered thing. It had two men in the cabin. When I looked with binoculars, people were getting off it. I increased the focus and light setting and saw a man looking back at me with a pair of binoculars."

"Creepy."

"It was, but in the next instant, Sarah Penhaligan came in with a takeaway and switched on the light. Naturally I couldn't see anything with the light on and by the time she switched it back off, the people and the man with the binoculars had disappeared."

"And you never saw these men again?"

"Oh, I think I did," he said. "I'm sure they were the two men who threatened me with the gun and attacked me."

"Why didn't you say this last night?"

O'Bryan scoffed. "I could tell he was a lousy copper. His line about Sarah told me that. As far as I was concerned, the woman had been sexually assaulted and taken against her will."

"I'm sure she's had worse."

O'Bryan looked at her. "I'm sure she has," he said seriously. "But there is always more to a situation than what can be seen at face value."

"I know, but…"

"No. That woman sells her body, that much is clear. I didn't see it coming, but I don't know any more than that," O'Bryan said. He looked at her, a feeling of uncertainty rising within him. Her comment had been callous. But then again, he'd thrown his hat into the ring with a woman he barely knew. He'd never done that before. What did he expect? He didn't even know DS Becky Hosking. If anything, he knew Sarah Penhaligan better. "Look, you clearly have history with this woman, other than nicking her for prostitution, so tell me."

"It's nothing," she answered curtly. "I knew of her when I holidayed down here. She was always knocking around Falmouth. I saw her around at the beaches, then when I was older, at the pubs and places older kids hang out. When I first nicked her it was awkward for her. A little for me too."

"And that's it?"

"I don't like people selling themselves," she added, "There's no need."

O'Bryan stepped out of the boat and DS Hosking scowled as she was left rocking and trying to stash the oars. "Need and want."

"What?"

"Everybody wants sex. It's a basic human emotion. We all want it for different reasons. To feel loved, to feel secure, to feel liberated. To feel in control, to feel dominated. Or just because it feels good," he said. "But in all my years as a police officer, I have never met anybody who truly wanted to sell their body for money. Not when you scratch away at the reasoning for doing it."

"Easy money."

"Is it? I'm sure if Brad Pitt came round and wanted to get his rocks off, the majority of women would jump at the chance…"

"Brad Pitt! You're showing your age!"

"Alright, that bloke off Poldark then," he said curtly. "But women in the sex industry don't get that. They get halitosis and missing teeth, fat and smelly beasts with hygiene problems and perverse desires.

They can't simply say no when they open the door to them."

She shrugged. "It's their career choice. Sarah Penhaligan could work on a supermarket checkout, but she chooses to spread her legs for a hundred quid a pop."

"I've known crime syndicates force women into that sort of work. There are immigrants who have their passports held and are forced to work for free to pay off the debt for being brought over. The sex industry is full of modern-day slaves with little choice."

"But Sarah has choices. She just makes bad ones, that's all." She pulled down the legs of her jeans and put the boots back on.

O'Bryan shrugged. He could see that history was unforgiving and made a note to delve deeper in Sarah Penhaligan's past. He would need the national crime database for the task, but he figured tomorrow would be the time for that. He had a meeting with Sarah at nine, he just hoped she would attend voluntarily.

"So what are we looking for?" DS Hosking asked, sensing it was time for a change in topic. "The boat brought people in, you say?"

"There were people on the jetty. All sizes. I only caught a fleeting glance. It could have been women or children. There were the two men who piloted the boat in."

"Smuggling, I'd bet," she said. "It goes on. Always has. It's just the booty that has changed. Drugs is the biggest and most valuable commodity. Everything from weed to ecstasy to cocaine. Drugs are rife in Cornwall."

"Really?"

"There's a big scene. Everybody smoked weed when I was a kid. Especially surfers and beach bums. Now it's as likely to be speed or ice. Heroin is in favour again."

O'Bryan shook his head. "I'd never have thought that."

"Cigarettes and tobacco is next, booze third. Vodka makes good sense. There are a lot of Polish here, they love the stuff. But pub landlords buy up anything and decant it into the branded optics. It's not so common now, not smuggled at least, because the budget supermarkets offer spirits so cheap, the landlords buy that instead. It goes on more than you'd think."

O'Bryan looked around, focusing his attention on the ground. There was a lot of mud and footprints. The jetty led to a path. The path looked well-used, like a coastal footpath, carved through the ground, but the wooden boards of the jetty were clean. One-way traffic. "Notice anything?"

DS Hosking studied the area. She looked at him and shook her head.

"The jetty is clean. People have moved in one direction. Or at least, a high proportion have."

She nodded. "Well, let's follow the path."

They walked single file, O'Bryan taking the lead. The path wound around the bank of the creek, then angled straight up a hill, so steep that O'Bryan could almost touch the ground in front of him. After fifty-metres or so the path went through a cluster of trees which gradually turned into a small wood. He turned to DS Hosking. "I thought they might have been poaching."

"Well this is Ogilvy's land, and the Malforth Estate hosts shoots."

"This is definitely his land?"

"Yes. It runs right down to the bank opposite Barlooe. That jetty has to be his."

"What do they shoot?"

"They breed and rear pheasants and drive them with beaters. I know people who have driven the birds for a part-time job. They stock deer as well. I think people pay to hunt them too."

"So it would be a worthwhile venture to sail up the river and shoot a deer. I suppose they are pretty big and could be butchered up and sold fairly easily. There was venison on the menu at The Smuggler's Rest. It would be worth selling it to kitchens via the backdoor."

"Absolutely," she said. "But you're not down from London to look into poaching and selling a bit of venison."

"No, I'm not."

"And the tie-in is the dead Syrian family."

"That's what I think."

She hesitated, her eyes catching something in the grass. Then she said quietly, "Oh Jesus…"

"What?"

"You know it's not smuggling don't you? Not contraband at least."

"That's what I'm going to prove."

"You think it's people trafficking, don't you," she stated flatly.

"I'm pretty sure it is, yes."

She walked off the path a few feet and bent down. She picked something up and walked over to him. She held it out and O'Bryan took it from her and looked at it. It was a tatty, worn teddy bear. Part of the arm had torn and stuffing was visible between the stretched threads and torn fabric. "I think you've found something," he said. He brought it close to his nose and smelled it, sniffing deeply. It smelled of something other than the woods, not yet taking on the musty, dank smell of the foliage and mud and grass.

It still smelled of its owner.

13

DS Hosking put the teddy in an evidence bag that she carried in her handbag. She marked the label with a marker pen. MM1. Malforth Manor, one. She dated it and put her name on it. She was about to enter O'Bryan's name, but he told her not to. She frowned, but he shook his head.

"I'm down here ruffling feathers," he said. "You take the credit." It was a good enough reason, but O'Bryan conceded it was not the only reason. But he couldn't tell her. Not yet.

"You think they trafficked children?"

He shook his head. "I think they trafficked a family."

"The Elmaleh family? You think they were being trafficked?"

"Not exactly…" he broke off, dropped to the ground as a huge clump of soil splattered over their faces and a gunshot sang out across the valley. It echoed sharply, unlike the gunshots he had heard previously during his stay.

"What the hell?" DS Hosking cried out. "Someone shot at us!"

There was another gunshot, another clump of soil. It was close to O'Bryan's feet. He rolled over and pulled DS Hosking down into a culvert. There were bones and animal fur in the culvert and it spread out from a large hole. O'Bryan realised it was a badger's sett.

"You there!" a voice called out. "What the hell are you doing on this land?"

O'Bryan chanced a peek and saw a tall, thin man dressed in tweed striding towards them. He was accompanied by a shorter, stockier man who wore a cheap and tatty green jacket and ripped jeans, which would have once been blue, but now looked the colour of mud.

The taller man carried a hunting rifle with a scope. The stockier man carried a shotgun, its barrels broken over his arm.

O'Bryan took out his warrant card and held it up. "Put the gun down!"

"I'll do nothing of the sort!" the taller man snorted. "Who the hell are you and what are you doing on Malforth Manor Estate?"

O'Bryan nodded for DS Hosking to get up. He turned to the men and said again, "Put the guns down. I'm a police officer, this is my colleague."

"You're trespassing without a warrant," the taller man said. "I'm Charles Ogilvy and I own this land."

"You shot at us," O'Bryan said. "Now put the guns down, or I'll take them off you."

The stockier man snapped the shotgun shut and the barrels drifted up towards O'Bryan's midriff. "No, I don't think you will…"

"Now, now Mitchell…" Ogilvy said. "I think we gave the inspector here a scare when we mistook him for a red hind on my land." He pulled back the bolt action and ejected a large brass cartridge into his hand. He rested the rifle on the ground at his feet. The man called Mitchell opened the barrels of the side by side shotgun and rested it in the crook of his elbow. He stared at O'Bryan, a smirk on his lips.

O'Bryan looked at the man's hands and forearms. Tattooed and tanned like the man holding the shotgun last night. The shotgun looked the same too. The blueing worn and shiny at end of the barrels. He looked at the man, watched his eyes carefully. He wasn't close enough to see if the iris of his right eye had bled into the white. "I didn't recognise you," he said. "Without your balaclava."

The man smiled. "Don't know what you mean, officer."

"I think you do."

Ogilvy coughed. "You know each other?"

Mitchell shook his head. "Never seen *he* before…"

"You sound the same."

"Well *we's* all sound the same to you *emmets*…"

O'Bryan looked at Ogilvy. "Mind if I take a look at your rifle?" He didn't wait for a reply, simply bent down and picked it up. He shouldered it and aimed at the point he had first seen the two men. He

118

lowered the rifle, looked back at Ogilvy. "That scope looks pretty clear to me. You must be half blind if you thought both DS Hosking and I looked like deer."

"You're a sergeant now?" Mitchell said with a smirk. "Well, the promotion ladder is open for women to climb here. They'll let anybody up, if *they's* give something in return, I *s'pose*."

"You shut your face! You odious little…"

"DS Hosking!" O'Bryan snapped. "That's enough…" He looked back at Ogilvy. "I was saying that you took two shots at people thinking they were a deer."

"Well, it's the light, you see," Ogilvy caught hold of the fore-stock and pulled, but O'Bryan gripped harder. "I didn't expect trespassers on my land."

"I think a visit from Firearms Licensing may be in order. Just to check you have everything in place. Like your DSC is valid. You need that to stalk deer, I gather."

"We run professional shoots here, Mitchell is in charge of all that."

Mitchell nodded. "Can't tell us a bloody thing…"

O'Bryan frowned and interrupted him. "Well, you thought I was a red hind. It's illegal to shoot female red deer this time of year. It's fallow deer and roe deer males in England and Wales. Just a quick

Google earlier. With such a simple mistake, I imagine you're making many more."

"I've only made one mistake lately," Mitchell said.

"You bet your life you have," O'Bryan said coldly. "And when you make another, I'll see it's the last you ever make…"

14

"Well, that could have gone better."

"I think it went pretty well myself," O'Bryan said. He stepped into the boat, eased himself to the back. "You're rowing, by the way."

"Naturally." She sat down on the jetty and eased herself down into the boat and onto the seat. The boat rocked, but O'Bryan was holding onto the edge of the jetty and it was far more stable than it had been both on the other side and in the middle of the creek. "And why didn't you mention the teddy bear?"

"Time and place. It wasn't looking too safe with the guns. And besides, if something is amiss, I want to hold the cards." He pushed away from the jetty once she got the oars into the water. "They shot at us on purpose. I saw the clarity of that rifle scope and it was a quality piece. If anything, they would have seen so much more than merely a figure moving. Ogilvy could have read the front page of a newspaper with that scope at that range."

"Are you sure it was the rifle that fired and not the shotgun?"

"Absolutely. The sound for one. And no spread pattern meant it was a bullet, not shotgun shot." O'Bryan looked at her as she rowed. "So what's with you and Mitchell? You know him. Or at least, he knows you and has an opinion of you."

"Remember I told you my ex took me apart in the courtroom and got a man off a rape charge? Well, that man was Pete Mitchell."

O'Bryan was silent for a moment, looked at her and said, "I'm convinced he was one of the men from last night. He had similar tattoos, from what I remember. The shotgun looked a match too, and he all but hinted as much. He thinks he's untouchable for some reason."

"That will be Ogilvy's influence."

"So who is he?"

"Sometime fisherman, now works as a gamekeeper and general dog's body for Ogilvy."

"And he was the one you were prosecuting? This was the case that cost you your relationship with your lawyer boyfriend?"

"No. It cost my lawyer boyfriend his relationship with me," she corrected him. "It showed me what a scumbag he was and what he would do to win his case."

"Okay. I get the differentiation." They were approaching the other side of the creek and O'Bryan nodded to her. "Twenty-feet, stop rowing."

She lifted the oars and the boat glided into the beach. There was a foot or so of mud and shingle to step onto. The boat was grounded and not going anywhere. O'Bryan, not caring for his filthy shoes and trouser bottoms, stepped out and into a few inches of water. DS Hosking started to unzip her boots, but he stopped her. "I'll lift you if you want," he said. "Save you messing about."

She looked up at him and shrugged. "Okay," she said and stood up.

O'Bryan bent down and put a hand behind her knees, the other around her waist and scissor motioned his arms. She dropped into his arms and looked up at him as he walked out of the water and onto the muddy beach. He looked at her, felt a quickening of his heartbeat as he watched her eyes. He swung her up to the top of the stone quay. She landed nimbly on the grass and he let go. The moment was gone and he bent down and lifted the prow of the boat up to the quay. "Here, take this," he said and walked around to lift the stern. She pulled and O'Bryan pushed and the boat slid neatly up the quay and rested still on the grass. The oars were inside. He'd turn the boat over and store it properly another time. For now, he wanted to change his trousers and shoes before he made his next port of call.

O'Bryan led the way through the garden and around the side of the house, letting them in through the front door. He dropped his keys onto the hall table and nodded towards the kitchen. "Get a brew on," he said, kicking his muddy shoes off. "How do you have your coffee?"

"Black," she said.

"Lucky. I haven't got any milk. I'll be down in a minute." He ran up the stairs and tore his trousers off at the top, took off his socks. He took out his wallet and warrant card, his mobile phone and pulled the belt out from the loops. He could hear DS Hosking filling the kettle, the water made some noise in the pipes, but he had never known pressure like it. The tap in the kitchen jumped each time it was shut off. He walked into the bedroom, dropped his things on the bed and took another pair of trousers out of the wardrobe. Dress was a little more casual in Cornwall, so he settled on a pair of tan cargoes and changed his shirt for a light blue one. He rolled the sleeves and wore it open one button down.

He had been quick, but by the time he got back down stairs, DS Hosking had the coffee made. She had taken it into the lounge and was watching the opposite river bank.

"We should move quickly," she said.

"We don't have anything concrete." He took the coffee off her and sipped a little, unsurprisingly, it was scalding.

"We have that teddy bear."

"Exactly."

"But with what you saw…"

"What *did* I see?" he paused. "Think as a lawyer. Would the teddy bear be enough for a warrant?"

She shook her head. "Okay, but we need to move. There could be a child, or an entire family…"

"Free because they paid to be brought over? It's how it could look, and it's not enough."

"What then?"

"Back to the Elmaleh family." O'Bryan perched on the back of the sofa and looked out across the water. The tide was still on the push. "I want to see them."

"What?" she asked, incredulously.

O'Bryan sipped some more coffee and kept his eyes on the glistening water of the creek. "Or more specifically," he paused. "I want to see their grave."

15

It was only five minutes longer than the most direct route through Falmouth, but at DS Hosking's suggestion, O'Bryan had taken the Castle Drive route and driven past Gyllyngvase Beach. With the stately-looking hotels to their right and a promenade overlooking the beautiful glistening sea to their left, it reminded O'Bryan of a short section of Torquay. He thought the sea view to be breath-taking, with sharp cliffs and smaller bays in the distance. Three large tankers were moored several miles out to sea. DS Hosking had told him that the promenade was an unusual feature in Cornwall, as she could only think of Penzance and Mount's Bay as having a promenade to walk along. They passed a sandy beach at the far end, a café and public garden, then the road left the beach behind and climbed through a residential area and DS Hosking told him to pull in and park on the left.

There were far worse places to be eternally laid to rest than the plots at Swanvale. Edged in trees, the plots set among neatly mowed grass, with plants growing sporadically and glimpsing views of the Atlantic Ocean, the site benefited from Falmouth's micro-climate of mild, bright weather all year round. DS Hosking informed O'Bryan that St. Ives and Falmouth had more hours of sun and were marginally warmer than anywhere else in Cornwall. She wasn't

126

wrong. The temperature was warmer than it had been back at Barlooe and the sun was high and the sky, cloud free.

O'Bryan got out of the car and looked at the main entrance. It was secured by black iron gates. There was a notice board and a list of contacts on the wall.

"Should have called," DS Hosking said.

"Now why didn't I think of that..." O'Bryan looked at the man approaching them. He was short and overweight, balding and wore the thickest glasses imaginable. Not the most fortunate fellow, but his smile was intoxicating and as warm as it was possible to be.

"Mister O'Bryan, sorry... Inspector?"

"That'll do," O'Bryan returned the man's smile and opened his warrant card for him to see. It indicated his newly reinstated rank of Detective Chief Inspector, but he wasn't going to go into ranks and protocols. "You must be Alan. Thank you for meeting with us, so late in the day."

"No, no. Always a pleasure to help the police," he said. "Actually, I've never really helped the police before, but it's still a pleasure!"

O'Bryan started walking into the burial gardens, prompting the man to follow and then assume the lead. "Did you not deal with the police after the vandalism to the grave?"

"No," he replied emphatically. "But I was given a log number."

"But nobody followed up with a visit?"

"No."

O'Bryan turned to DS Hosking as they walked in the shade of the tree canopies. "Was there talk about the incident?" he asked.

"I didn't hear anything. No investigation as far as I know. The papers ran with the story for a while, but I didn't hear of any police action." She ducked a branch and swiped a lock of hair from her face. "There are around a hundred officers in CID throughout Cornwall. We work out of whichever station is geographically closest to the crime. With many stations closing in favour of non-emergency calls direct to Exeter, we don't rub shoulders too regularly. There are officers I don't see from one month to the next and some I'll never see. We don't get to hear much concerning other cases. Most contact is through email and our internal online bulletin board."

They rounded the path and entered a garden edged in privet bush. Alan stopped, his head bowed. They stopped too, O'Bryan bowed his head in mutual respect, noticed DS Hosking looked towards the sea. "Here we are," Alan said quietly.

The plot was covered in fresh earth and there were flowers on top in a sunken vase. They looked fresh, but O'Bryan didn't know what they were. The headstone looked to be marble or polished granite. He suspected the latter given the amount of granite he had seen throughout the county.

"So you cleaned the headstone off?" O'Bryan asked.

"No, there was no damage to the headstone, detective," Alan sighed. "The people from the Islamic centre at Carnon Downs came down and replaced the vase. They replenished the flowers and the Imam held a sort of blessing."

"But the headstone wasn't touched?"

"No."

"What was the extent of the vandalism?" O'Bryan frowned. "Just the broken vase?"

Alan shook his head. "No, I didn't really say it was vandalism," he said, somewhat perplexed. "I said that whoever had done this had tried to dig the grave out properly."

DS Hosking pulled a face. It wasn't the prettiest she'd looked all day. "You mean…"

"Yes!" exclaimed Alan. "That's what I said to the other detective. It was as though someone tried to get to the bodies."

"But you said that you didn't deal with the police. You never said you spoke to someone," O'Bryan sighed. "Which is it?"

"I didn't speak to anyone in person," he said. "I called the police when we discovered the damage. I was given a log number." He took out a fold of paper and handed it to O'Bryan. "Here," he said. "It's all on there, date, number and time."

"Right…"

"The other warden who worked here spoke to the police when they came," he said.

"And what did they say?"

"It was just one officer, a detective. He looked around, took some photographs and told John he'd better fill it back in. We called the Westbriton newspaper and they came out and took a picture of the Islamic charity replacing the flowers. We'd filled it in by then. Couldn't have an open grave for all the world to see…"

"Well, how far did they dig down?"

"Four feet or so."

"Four feet!" O'Bryan shook his head. "Well that wasn't just petty vandalism. That would have been damned hard work, organised too."

"I know, that's what we said. John came in early, saw the gates had been broken open and a great van was parked outside. He heard noise inside and went in to take a look."

O'Bryan shook his head. It wasn't the most sensible thing he'd heard. But it wasn't the worse. "How early?" O'Bryan asked.

"About five. John was up with the lark. He would do a few chores here then go back to Flushing and go out in his boat, set his crab and lobster pots or bring in the ones he'd had soaking. Then he'd come back and work part of the day. We keep our hours quite flexible. He shouted at them and obviously disturbed them while they were digging. He said they'd had a scuffle, but I think he exaggerated a bit. He must have chased them off though."

"So can you give me his number? I think it's high time I got his version of events."

Alan cast his head for a moment. He looked back at both of them and shrugged. "I'm sorry, John Turner had an accident. He got caught up with one of his pots and fell overboard," he said sadly. "He was a typical fisherman, not a great swimmer, but he must have snared his leg in the line or something, because he was pulled overboard and under the surface."

"When was this?" DS Hosking asked. She glanced at O'Bryan, then looked back at the small, round man.

"The day after."

They were silent for a moment. Alan out of respect for his dead colleague, O'Bryan and DS Hosking because of what question was to be asked next.

"Was this reported to the police?" O'Bryan asked.

Alan shrugged. "No idea. A passing fishing boat brought him in. Another crabbing boat that berths in Flushing."

"Thank you Alan," O'Bryan said. "I've got your number; I'll call if I need anything else."

Alan took his cue and nodded. "Pleasure," he said and walked back the way they had come.

"What are you thinking?" DS Hosking asked.

"What are *you* thinking, sergeant?"

"I thought I said call me Becky," she said.

"Okay, Becky. What are you thinking?"

"I think it's a possibility that John Turner recognised the people, or at least one of the people digging up the grave."

O'Bryan nodded. "I think it's more like one of them recognised *him*, and couldn't take the chance that Turner hadn't recognised them."

"We definitely think Turner's death is related though," she said flatly.

"We do."

"We need to look into his death then. I'd heard a man had drowned, a fisherman. But it was a snippet on the late night local news. No *real* story. It happens quite a lot down here."

"It's not the only thing though."

"What else is there?"

O'Bryan looked down at the grave, the fresh earth, the new flowers and the undamaged headstone. "We don't know for sure if the men digging were actually digging up a grave," he paused. "Or whether they were filling an *empty* grave back in."

16

"What do we do next?" DS Hosking asked as O'Bryan parked and switched off the engine.

The harbourmaster's office was directly ahead of them. They did not have an appointment, but O'Bryan figured there would be someone around who could point them in the right direction. He tapped the steering wheel with his fingers, nibbled the inside of his cheek. It was anxiety, and it came on when he needed a drink.

Sixty-days...

The cruel irony was that he didn't miss the taste of it. But needed it instead to quell a host of emotions and irregularities within him - from breathing, to thinking, even to his equilibrium. It was as if the alcohol diluted something, balanced him out. Like the fuel to air mixture of an engine's carburettor. He knew when he felt like this, he would function better, in the short-term, with a drink. However, he also knew it merely greased a dangerous slope, that if stepped on, would not halt his descent until he reached rock bottom.

"Did you hear me, Ross?" she prompted.

"Sorry," he said. "Just thinking."

"What do we do next?"

"Let's see what happens here first."

"But the grave," she said. "What if you're right? What if they got to the bodies and were in fact filling the grave back in?"

"That's not the immediate question."

"What?"

"There's a bigger question."

She frowned. "What could be a bigger question than: *are the bodies still in the grave?*"

"We know that there's probably a fifty-fifty chance they're not."

"Really?" She leaned back in her seat, the sun bright across her face. "I'd say there's a bigger chance they are still in the grave. It's a lot of work to dig out five bodies, take them elsewhere, presumably to a vehicle, then refill."

"But they didn't finish refilling, if they started at all."

"So what's the bigger question?"

He looked at her intently. "Why?" he said. "Why would they dig, or attempt to dig them up?"

"Anti-Islamic fuck-wits. Maybe they don't need a reason."

"Oh, they need a reason. And I think the reason is because they were buried. The majority of people are cremated these days. But Muslims request burial, and they need it within twenty-four hours. Now, the Elmaleh family didn't make this, unfortunately. But the Islamic community stepped in and paid for the plot and sought to get the ceremony performed and had them buried soon after. Now, they were found drowned, and the cause of death confirmed this. I have seen the post-mortem, and I have to say for a family washed up on the beach with the wreckage of their boat and the whole sorry immigrant crisis story around them, as well as pressure from the Islamic community to get them in the ground ASAP, possibly with a little departmental influence to avoid an ethnic or racial situation, then I suppose the coroner's report is about right," he paused. "But there was no indication of foul play. So the bodies were released to the Islamic charity that paid for the family plot, and that should have been an end to it."

"So, why do you think someone wanted them…" She searched for the words, but shrugged lamely. "…dug up?"

"I think my boss made a few enquiries and spooked someone. Someone who is in the know, on the inside. He wasn't happy with something, and other than staying for a period of illness and recovery in his family holiday home at Barlooe, I don't know what else would have prompted him to look into it."

"He's ill?"

O'Bryan thought of Anderson, the man's death still raw. Thirty-six hours. O'Bryan cursed inwardly at his date with Sarah Penhaligan and missing the first time and date in the calendar. He had wasted precious time. The thought of the teddy bear

DS Hosking had found made him want to retch. Had he started to investigate sooner, could he have stopped what he assumed to be a movement of people? "Kind of," he said. "Not anymore though," he paused thoughtfully and added, "I think the Elmaleh family were murdered. And I think whoever did it was convinced that their deaths would look to all the world like misadventure and they would be cremated. The line of evidence would be severed totally. Now, the commander of Special Branch has an inkling and starts a private inquiry. It causes a panic, because somebody in the know hears of it. That prompts them to get the bodies before there is a chance of official exhumation and a thorough, detailed autopsy from the inside out."

"And poor John Turner recognised them?"

"No. I think *they* recognised John Turner and weren't sure if he had recognised them, so they killed him before he could talk. Or at least work it out."

"You think they drowned him?" she asked. "Made it look like an accident?"

"Fits the MO of the Elmaleh family."

"Jesus…" she shook her head.

O'Bryan opened his door. "Come on," he said. "Let's see if the harbourmaster can shed any light on it."

It was actually the Falmouth Harbour Commissioners Office. And the man in charge was Martin Gwennap. Judging from his movements, his

136

physique and eyes, O'Bryan put him in his forties but his face was as weathered and tanned as a crocodile's back. He sported a neatly trimmed greying beard and was wearing an inflatable life-vest, though uninflated, and wore a two-way radio on a strap across his vest. He also wore a fisherman's knife and a multi-tool in a pouch on his belt.

"I dealt with it personally," he said in reply to O'Bryan's question regarding John Turner's death.

"You discovered the body?"

Gwenapp shook his head. "Not like that," he said, his Cornish as broad as his shoulders. "I answered the distress call, met the boat on its way back in."

"The boat that found him?"

"Yes. I set aside an area on the quay, called the ambulance, but they weren't needed by the time they brought him in."

"He was alive when they found him?"

"Don't think so, but you always call an ambulance as a matter of course."

O'Bryan nodded. "So the body went to...?"

"Treliske Hospital," he said. "There wasn't an inquest. Turner was seventy-years old and fell overboard pulling in his crab pots. It's dangerous work. The man had got himself caught up with the rope. I imagine he gulped a breath in panic and that's all it takes to start drowning."

"That's it? No coroner, no post-mortem?"

Gwenapp shrugged. "He was a fisherman. Even in summer, once you're a mile or so off shore the water is freezing cold. He's wearing jeans and wellington boots, a jacket and no life vest. He was seventy and like most fishermen, he wasn't much of a swimmer. You take's your chances."

"Is he buried around here? Swanvale perhaps?" O'Bryan cursed not asking Alan while he was up there.

"No. Cremation at Penmount," he said. "Up the other side of Truro. Small service. I attended, I didn't really know him, but you know..." he shrugged.

O'Bryan did know. He had attended more than a few services for people he did not know, but had been a part of the investigation into their death. He had gone to a few to watch the crowd as well. Killers loved to go to their victim's funeral.

"Who found the body?" DS Hosking asked.

Gwenapp turned to her. "Local chap, does a bit of potting and long-lining. Not regular, like. He used to but now works as a handyman and gamekeeper nearby. Over at Malforth Manor. He keeps a boat in Flushing too. Knew John Turner well."

"What's his name?" O'Bryan asked, a tingle running up his spine. He already knew the answer.

"Mitchell. Pete Mitchell," the harbourmaster said. "He was at the service too."

17

"I've never signed an exhumation order before."

"Few have."

"But why don't you want to do it?"

"I don't want it to be blocked."

"Who is going to do that?"

"Someone might," O'Bryan paused. "There is a *someone* working against justice here, somebody with an ear to the ground and an eye on the law."

"Who do you suspect?"

"Well, we need to find out who visited the Swanvale burial site, because clearly more action could have been taken."

"That shouldn't be too difficult," DS Hosking commented. She watched the road ahead and said, "Next left."

O'Bryan slowed and took the left off the mini-roundabout. They had driven on the Falmouth bypass and were heading back towards Camborne police station. He needed to log into the police database and make some checks. He also needed a good internet connection to search for a few things. He wanted DS Hosking to see to exhuming the bodies, or simply confirming that they were actually still in the ground. If they were, then he wanted a Home Office pathologist to perform an in depth autopsy on the Syrian family. That was not as easy as it sounded. He was hoping that a detective sergeant would have enough clout to set the ball rolling. But he didn't know Cornwall and its procedure. And he didn't want to make the case high-profile. He had instructed DS Hosking to over-play an obvious race card from the start. A dead family deserved justice, would an exhumation not be granted quicker if the family were white? Exhumation is a sacrilegious act in Islam, so perhaps it should be done quietly and without unnecessary obstruction or procedure. If this was to be refused, was it a race thing? Nine out of ten times people wouldn't want to be involved in any of that. They would be susceptible to bending with the pressure.

"You need to play it," O'Bryan said. "And you need to make it clear that the damage done to their grave indicated potential, or actual body snatching and that we are not certain whether or not this has been achieved."

"I'll get it done," she said.

O'Bryan found himself driving through Lanner and onwards down into Redruth. Strangely, with the sun on it and a blue sky, it looked a little less grey and depressing. He commented on this to DS Hosking.

"It's all granite around here. And Carn Brea, the big hill and monument over there," she said and pointed at a hill which must have been just short of a mountain, "It seems to suck in the cloud and make it all grey and damp. To be fair, it's never usually bright and sunny like this around here."

"Well, it's a *little* less depressing than this morning," he commented flatly.

It was cloudy and grey in Camborne. But this was Cornwall and the weather was different every few miles you travelled. O'Bryan had read that it was something to do with being a narrow peninsular meeting the weather patterns from the Atlantic. The Gulfstream current warmed the water and the Airstream was meant to sweep in and blow north of Cornwall. In recent years, the Airstream had shifted and that had left Cornwall with cooler, wetter summers. As if a place with such unsettled weather needed worse summers. O'Bryan couldn't complain though, he hadn't seen rain for his entire stay, and the early evenings always seemed sunny and mild regardless of cloud or breeze in the daytime.

He parked the Alfa Romeo in a narrow space and squeezed out of his half-open door. He saw DCI Trevithick getting into an unmarked Ford Focus at the other end of the carpark. O'Bryan raised a hand, not for a greeting, but to indicate that he wanted to speak to him, but the car shot out of the carpark and turned left.

"I don't think he wanted to speak to you," DS Hosking said sardonically.

"You don't say," O'Bryan replied.

DS Hosking led the way and opened the door with a swipe card and a four-digit code. "You'll need one of these," she said. "I'll speak to the duty officer and set you up."

"Thanks."

"So, I'll call the coroner and get something in progress before knocking off," she said. "Unless there's anything else?"

"No, that's fine. Do I need anything to log on?"

"Yes. I'll sort you out with the password." She led the way through to the CID suite and the ginger-haired detective with the greying beard looked up as they entered. He said nothing, turned back to his screen. She leaned over a desk in front of O'Bryan and tapped on the keyboard. "That should be okay. Unless you want to take the boss's office?"

O'Bryan shook his head. "This'll do," he said. He felt he had made his point earlier. "When you get my pass card and give me the pass-code, ask the duty officer to arrange an office for me with a computer terminal. I'll be back in for eight-thirty tomorrow morning, there must be a space somewhere they can shoe-horn me in."

She looked a little shocked, but nodded. "I'll get onto it now, Ross," she said, then glanced at the detective who had looked up. "I mean, *Superintendent*."

"Great," he said and sat down at the desk. He didn't look back up and she left to talk to the desk officer. He looked up when she was outside the suite. "Detective," he said.

"Yes, sir. Detective Sergeant Harris," he said. "Chris Harris."

"DS Harris, do you know where DCI Trevithick has gone? Or when he is planning on getting back?"

"I think he's knocking off duty, sir."

He won't be back, thought O'Bryan. *Still licking his wounds...*

O'Bryan looked at his watch. It was an oversized Omega Seamaster on a black rubber strap, and was precious to him. He had won it in his final year of university in an international water polo match sponsored by the watch maker. The entire winning team had been awarded one. He had pawned it once to pay for booze, a rock bottom moment, and he was lucky enough to have managed to buy it back when he had reached one-hundred days' sobriety. Each time he looked at it, he knew he could make it. And this time, he would.

The time was five-fifteen. It wasn't an unreasonable time to punch out, it depended upon what investigation was in progress. He knew that Trevithick would have put in more than a few twenty-hour shifts in his time, he wouldn't have made DCI if he hadn't, but he suspected that DCI Trevithick had merely wanted to make himself scarce. He couldn't blame him, but he had more than a few questions for the man when he came back in.

"Right, all done," DS Hosking said, walking in with a file. "You'll have the broom cupboard next door." She smiled. "Joke. There's an interview room that's going to get a makeover in the next hour or so. Should be serviceable by the time you come in tomorrow."

"Great," O'Bryan smiled. "Did you catch the coroner?"

"I did. He's going to be working until six, but he said he'd check his emails at home every hour or so until about ten. So he'll evaluate the report and email me back."

"Was he… open to the request?"

"I think so. He agreed we need to know whether they are actually still in the ground or not. That's a given. It should be signed by the morning. He didn't hint as to whether we'd get the autopsy if they were still there, we need to find that out first. But he agreed we don't want to have to fill it in, merely to dig it all out again, but he wanted to get a second opinion on it first and would forward our report on. I explained our findings and our doubt as to any conclusion of misadventure." She looked up as DS Harris walked past them without a word, she frowned at his apparent rudeness. From the way he was putting on his jacket, it was clear he was leaving his shift.

144

"Sorry, where was I? Oh, yes... First we get confirmation, but it would be worth calling him as soon as we discover whether or not they are there." She shivered. "Creepy, isn't it? I mean, laid to rest and then some monster digs you up, for Lord knows what purpose..."

O'Bryan had his theories, but he didn't share them with her. Better to wait and see if there would be an in depth autopsy. "Well, get our findings and theories down and email him as soon as you've finished."

"Okay," she said and went over to her work station. She pulled out her chair and sat down heavily.

O'Bryan logged onto the computer and made the searches he required on the police database. He opened the browser and started to search the internet, then flicked between the open tabs. He jotted on a notepad and occasionally saved documents or internet URL's to his personal cloud. He would be able to access them later from his laptop. He worked solidly for twenty-minutes, then looked up as DS Hosking stood up and pushed her chair under the desk.

"I'm done," she said.

"You sent it?"

"I have," she replied. "Do you want to see what I've sent?"

He wasn't one to micro-manage. She was an experienced DS. "No," he said. "I'll see you back here in the morning. I'm interviewing Sarah

Penhaligan about the assault at nine-thirty." He noted she looked disinterested. "Leave tomorrow free, you can assist me again."

"Really?" she smiled.

"Yes."

"Alright," she said, a little coyly. "I'll see you in the morning."

O'Bryan returned to his screen and worked for another twenty-minutes. He was satisfied that the CID suite would not be in use for the rest of the day. He shut down his computer and glanced down the corridor before heading to search DCI Trevithick's office.

18

O'Bryan dropped the keys onto the kitchen table and opened the fridge. He needed to go to a shop. He knew it would be empty, but it was a force of habit. He realised he was going to be staying longer than he had initially anticipated. There were two bottles of wine at the back. They were screw top sauvignon blanc. Next to them were European mini bottles of beer, which he thought had been German, but now suspected Czech Republic. He hesitated, he should have picked up some groceries. He closed the door and picked up the kettle. Anderson had a fancy Italian coffee machine installed into a recess in the wall, but O'Bryan had tried and failed to get it working. He filled the kettle, put it back on its base and took a sachet of coffee and a cafetiere out of the cupboard. He looked back at the kettle, then opened the fridge again. The beer and the wine were still there. He had resisted temptation before. He had dramatically poured all the alcohol down the sink in an act of finality, back when his wife had failed to support him and continued to buy it for herself and entertaining their friends, who had later all become *her* friends. But he knew that the act of ridding himself of the alcohol was one thing and the simplicity of driving to an all-night supermarket in the early hours was another. Whether he got rid of the drink or let it remain in the fridge calling to him didn't matter.

There was always access and he needed to overcome the urge. He took out his wallet and slipped out the photograph of his daughter Chloe. The photograph was creased and worn, it had been unfolded and looked at daily. She was laughing, sitting on a pony at a petting farm. O'Bryan stood one side, and the photo had been folded, in a darker time, to hide his wife, who was standing on the other side. A snapshot of a happy family, unaware of the torment and misery, the disappointment and rawness of the split that lay ahead of them. He looked at the woman in the photograph, now his ex-wife. She had once been pretty and kind, but he had taken all of that away, eroded it to a husk. She would never love him again, and nor did he feel he deserved her love for that matter. In his darker hours, he would blame her for not giving him her support, for not accepting his alcoholism as an illness and fighting it alongside him as one would with something more tangible like a cancer, but ultimately he knew the fight was always his and his alone. He had put too much weight on her, and more besides. She had played her part too, but his condition would always have been the catalyst. He still wasn't ready to unfold her, probably never would, but he would never tear the photograph and remove her presence altogether. She needed to be there as a permanent reminder, a spectre of regret. Because without regret, there would never be hope or fulfilment.

The kettle switched off, seemingly boiling faster because of the distraction, and he made the coffee, poured it into an oversized mug and walked through to the lounge. The sun was low, almost touching the hill far beyond the creek and casting a golden hue on the water's surface. The tide was full and with little wind, the water looked like a mirror.

He drank a good mouthful of coffee and placed the cup down on the top of the bookcase, before opening the sliding glass doors. He took off his clothes, keeping his boxer shorts on. His heartrate quickened, there was an underlying panic he did his best to quell, but he knew he needed to do it, and he had already proved he was no oarsman in the rowing boat with DS Hosking earlier.

O'Bryan stepped out onto the grass and it was soft and warm underfoot. He walked the length of the garden and looked at the surface of the water, saw the depth of the mud and stones underneath. He estimated it was a little less than a metre. He looked each way, to the neighbouring property on his right, and to the grass-topped quay and area of grass to his left. There was nobody on the footpath, nobody anywhere in sight. He closed his eyes, saw the face in his dreams, the face of his nightmares. The water was no longer the same for him, but he must try to suppress his anxiety. He had been brilliant once, a phenomenal swimmer and diver. He felt a little less anxious and knew that it was now or never.

O'Bryan leaped and shallow dived into the water. His chest and stomach scraped the bottom and sent up a great cloud of silt. He chanced opening his eyes and saw several flat fish darting off in front of him. The water was cool, but not unpleasant and he stroked hard, crawling and alternating his intake of breath under each arm, blowing a clear stream of bubbles with his head straight for three strokes. He could no longer see the bottom, the visibility was only around three-feet or so. He looked straight ahead, his eyes stinging from the salt and kept his focus on the jetty. He was halfway across and the current was negligible. He figured it was just about on high tide.

As he approached the jetty, he could see more and the water was deeper. He was not entirely sure why the visibility was better here, but when he finally reached the jetty, he took a breath and dropped down, pushing his feet towards the bottom. The water was noticeably colder and he estimated it to be around ten-feet deep.

O'Bryan pulled himself out of the water and sat for a moment on the jetty. The sun was still visible, the rays warming him, but as he got up and walked to the path, the shade was cold and unforgiving. The ground was slippery underfoot, but he shortened his stride and made good progress. He was soon in the place where both he and DS Hosking had been shot at. The place where she had found the teddy bear.

Now starting to shiver, O'Bryan entered the wooded area. There was movement around him, scuffling and digging and the sound of birds darting through the undergrowth. His presence did not seem to scare them away. The ground ahead of him rose and there were granite boulders of varying sizes from football-sized fragments through to the size of family hatchbacks. After a few more paces, he realised that this must have been the distance and area from which Charles Ogilvy had taken his two shots at them. He turned around and surveyed the area he had come from. Even without the rifle scope, he was convinced that Ogilvy would have been able to see that they were people and not deer. So why would Ogilvy have risked shooting? Why take the chance? O'Bryan walked back the way he had come and stepped back onto the path. He continued on the route that both he and DS Hosking would have taken. The huge slabs of granite piled up on both sides, funnelling the pathway and then the area opened out into a clearing. At the far end of the clearing he could see a gap in the granite. As he walked closer, he could see that it was a cave entrance. The light was fading fast, and with it the temperature felt as if it had plummeted. Standing in only the pair of damp, white boxer shorts, O'Bryan was cold and felt vulnerable. He glanced around him, then stepped into the cave entrance. It was pitch black, but just a few feet inside, he could see the heavy metal bars of a pair of double wrought iron gates. He caught hold of them and gave the structure a shake. It was solid, but rattled in the middle. He felt along and could see that there was a half-inch gap where the two sections of bars met. A large padlock, as big as his fist shackled two rings, fastening them in place. He ran his hands over the edges nearest the stone wall and could feel enormous hinges set at three intervals.

O'Bryan stood back. He had heard of such smuggling tunnels. There was even a black and white picture and short paragraph framed on the wall of The Smuggler's Rest pub across the water in Barlooe. Used in the late seventeen-hundreds and early eighteen-hundreds by smugglers and wreckers to hide their bounty, there had been several discovered over the years. O'Bryan assumed that Malforth Manor had such a concession going on two-hundred years ago. The rum and tobacco would have been brought in by boat coinciding with the appropriate tides and cover of darkness, perhaps even with the right amount of moonlight, and the contraband would be divvied up and walked out of the doors of the manor house and onto horse and carts for distribution across Cornwall, maybe even to London where it could buy influence. Things hadn't changed over the years, but it was the thought of what may be being smuggled that left O'Bryan cold, and not just the night time air. He looked down at the ground in the cave entrance. It was worn enough to have had multiple people passing through its entrance for a while.

There was nothing more he could do here, so he made his way back down the pathway, stopping occasionally when he heard movement in the undergrowth. Paranoia was getting the better of him and he was relieved when he reached the jetty. It was almost completely dark now, save for the golden strip of light above the distant hill at the far end of the valley. To his right, down the creek and towards the sea, it was dark and he could see the lights of Point Geddon in the distance. He looked across the water, but could not see the Hemingway House, as he had forgotten to leave a light on. He cursed his lack of thought. But for his money, it was a direct swim straight out from the jetty. He closed his eyes, already seeing the face and the vision he so often felt recently when he looked at water.

It's all in the past, all in your mind...

He dived off the edge of the jetty and stroked powerfully out into the creek. He breathed to his right, every six strokes, a technique he used for powerful bursts to put on a good speed and distance. He didn't hesitate, merely kept up the pace. After a dozen or so breaths, he glanced up and realised he was way off course. He had drifted a long way down river and he panicked for a moment as he treaded water and searched for the house. It was a hundred-metres further up-river and he changed course and swam as hard as he could. After several minutes of ploughing onwards, he raised his head to find he had made no progress whatsoever, and he felt a rush of fear within him, his heartbeat beating from both the exertion and panic. He aimed for the bank now and started to breast stroke, as his breathing was off and he was too tired to front-crawl. For the first time since the incident in London, the wounded muscle in both his shoulder and torso gave him pain, akin to sharp bursts like cramp. He made a little progress, but Barlooe was passing by and he was heading down to Point Geddon. At the quay, the creek veered right sharply and it was open water all the way out into the Carrick Roads. Panic was with him now, and he started to snatch his breath. For the first time in his life, he was genuinely fearful he would drown. He took a huge breath, dipped his head and made a last surge for the bank. After perhaps thirty strokes, he raised his head and saw a figure running in pace with him on the footpath. Part of his subconscious mind marvelled on the speed in which he was being pulled out to sea. A more useful part of his mind saw the buoy the person threw and thankfully, realised they had thrown it well down river from him. He breast-stroked hard, watching the buoy bob on the surface. He snatched at it and missed. His heart sunk, but he kicked and stroked hard and caught hold, gripping for dear life. He continued to kick, felt the rope go tight and felt himself stop dead in the current, which now pulled at him harder, putting a great deal of tension on the rope. He prayed they could pull him in, but he aided the effort by clutching the buoy close and using his left hand to stroke and kicked wildly with both legs. He could see the bank getting closer and after a dozen strokes and twenty-feet or so, he felt the bottom with tired feet. He righted himself, and waded against the current, feeling the tautness of the rope anchoring him upright and bringing him steadily in.

As he reached the bank he collapsed, exhausted. His legs were still in the water, and he felt the current wash over his skin. He struggled upwards and rolled over onto his back, heaving for breath and a warm rush of euphoria enveloping him like a warm blanket. After a full minute, he looked up at the person who had undoubtedly saved him.

"Jesus, Ross," Sarah Penhaligan said. "You were doing well up until you hit the middle of the creek. But that's where the river is running permanently, whether the tide's coming in, dropping or slack." She smiled, a thick lock of red hair slipped down across her face and she swiped it aside and tucked it behind her ear. "You're like most emmets," she said. "You could swim all day in a pool, but you don't know shit about the tides and *real* swimming…"

19

O'Bryan wasn't quite walking wounded, but he was able to lean on Sarah as she walked with him along the riverbank, without feeling that he was acting unduly dramatic. She was warm and he could feel the heat coming off her. He was shivering uncontrollably by the time they reached the garden and walked through the welcoming doors of the house.

Sarah closed the glass doors and drew the curtains. She took a throw off the leather sofa and wrapped it around him. "Hot shower for you," she said. "You're bordering on hypothermic."

He would have agreed, had his teeth not been chattering so much, she put an arm around him and guided him up the stairs and into the bathroom. The shower was a double cubicle and had three jets, one large ceiling rose and two more from the sides. The water was heated by a gas combi-boiler, and the heat was instant. O'Bryan stepped in and the water burned and stung like pins and needles. Sarah placed a towel on the heated towel rail.

"Thank you," he stammered slightly. He couldn't imagine himself getting out of the water once he had drifted past Point Geddon. He would surely have drowned. He looked at her sheepishly. "I think you just saved my life," he said meekly.

She smiled, leaned into the shower and kissed him on the cheek, her hair getting wet with spray. He knew what she had done earlier that day, what she was, but there was an innocence in her eyes, and an infectiousness to her manner that made him look past it all. "You're welcome," she said. "Perhaps you can save mine." She didn't smile, or add *someday* to the sentence as banter. She said it seriously, and he looked back at her with concern.

"Sarah…"

She cut him off before he could continue. "Coffee!" she said. "I'll get some on. You need to warm from the inside too." She hovered at the door. "I can get another Chinese delivery, if you want to try again. We've got the life-threatening situation out of the way first tonight. What can go wrong?" She didn't give him the chance to answer and closed the door after her.

O'Bryan felt his core warming. The water had been tolerable, but he knew it was the shock and exertion that had knocked it out of him. The hot coffee would help, and he was ravenous now that Sarah had mentioned food. He could almost taste and smell the aroma of a Chinese takeaway.

He switched off the cascades of hot water and stepped carefully out onto the tiled floor. The window and mirrors had steamed like a sauna and he could barely see across the room to the door. He rubbed the condensation away from the cabinet mirror and looked at himself. He was convinced he was going to die. He had felt the same way twice before and for

157

some reason staring at himself in the mirror was a comfort. As if it were a chance to both condemn and praise himself, celebrate his evasion of the alternative to what he was seeing now. His reflection was confirmation of his survival.

O'Bryan dressed in the master bedroom. Jeans and a sweatshirt. He was warmed through, and now he just wanted to slouch. He couldn't remember feeling so exhausted. He thought about Sarah and how he had seen her earlier today. Dressed for a performance. Now she was the girl next door, in jeans and a tight-fitting T-shirt, a cardigan over her shoulders. She had run quickly down the quay and the footpath along the riverbank. He hadn't noticed her footwear, but suspected she wore trainers. So different from when he had seen her in the leather dress that had barely covered her dignity and the ridiculous heels which had brought her up to his own height. But it had all seemed part of an act. She hadn't been comfortable, and O'Bryan sensed that this was the real Sarah Penhaligan and he wanted to know more about her and the choices she had made in life.

As he walked down the staircase he could hear Sarah in the kitchen. She was preparing something, the sound of the microwave and the fan oven, of the cutlery drawer opening. O'Bryan knew he did not have any food in the house and thought that mentioning another takeaway was more of a joke than a possibility. Perhaps she had brought some food with her, or had stopped by after shopping for some and decided to share. He was famished after the swim, needed to eat and wasn't about to put up an argument.

"Sorry to have interrupted, but I think I might have saved you again," DS Hosking said, reaching two plates out of the cupboard.

O'Bryan recoiled when he saw her, then gradually regained some composure. "Where's Sarah?" he managed to say, almost casually.

"I sent her packing," she said. "Mind you, perhaps I was too late?" She laughed as she opened a microwave ready meal and started to spoon rice and chicken korma onto both of the plates. "I mean, she had wet hair, and you've just got out of the shower. Mate's rates? Or did she charge full whack? What is that by the way? Must be at least thirty-quid…"

O'Bryan glared. "It wasn't like that," he protested. He watched her spoon something red on the plate, tikka he thought. It smelled good. "She *saved* me, actually."

"From what, a night of abstinence?"

"From drowning."

"Seriously? I thought you were a good swimmer, you know, from what they said in the papers…" she trailed off.

O'Bryan walked over and picked up some naan bread. It was steaming. He dipped it in the red sauce and took a bite. "I swam over and took a look at the ground on Malforth Estate."

"What? Ross, they shot at us last time!"

"I swam over and it was okay. On the way back I hit a bad current and missed the bank. Actually, I missed Barlooe completely and nearly missed Point Geddon. If Sarah hadn't thrown me a line, I think I would have gone right on past The Pandora and out to sea…"

"Jesus…" she said, but wasn't compelled enough to stop dishing up the meal.

"What did you say to her?" he asked. He owed Sarah more than the short shrift from a colleague he had only known for twenty-four hours.

"I just told her to go." She shrugged. "Look, Ross, I don't know what you've got going on with her. But I'm surprised you'd have *anything* to do with her after finding out what she is today. But if you don't mind that, then I'll butt out. We'll forget all about our drink or whatever after this, if you don't mind… But she's bad news. She falls in and out of love with the wrong people, she's a train wreck socially, financially, in every conceivable area."

O'Bryan nodded. "She saved me tonight. And she said I might be able to *save* her. I've seen a lot of women do what she does, but I have never met one who should do it less. There's something not right about why she does it. But regardless of that, she genuinely saved my life tonight. I owe her, and that's reason enough for you to *butt out*, as you say."

"Fine. Fill your boots." She snatched up her handbag and made for the door. O'Bryan had seen this before. He'd seen it in every relationship he'd ever had. Maybe it was him. She would stop and have the last word before she left. And the last word was always the most cutting. "I just hope you have enough money to pay for what I would have given for free…" She was genuinely tearful as she wrenched open the door and slammed it behind her.

O'Bryan picked up a plate and a fork and started to eat. DS Becky Hosking's words were nothing to him. He had liked her, fallen a little bit for her in a day, but she had shown him something more to her character. He didn't believe that her bad feeling towards Sarah Penhaligan was down to the fact the woman had sold sex. There had to be more. O'Bryan had fallen out of his little crush in less time than it took to dish up a chicken korma. But what worried him most was that she had not asked anything about what he had done, or what he had discovered on the Malforth Estate. She had concentrated only on Sarah. There was so much more to her dislike of her, but right now, he was too tired and hungry to think.

20

The office was windowless and oppressive. There was a computer and monitor rigged up with access to the mainframe, server and national police database. He had a telephone and a printer. Someone had even left a few pens, pencils and a notepad on the desk.

"We've got our exhumation," DS Hosking said, hovering in the doorway, her body wrapped around the doorframe. She did not show any animosity from last night. No emotion whatsoever.

"You surprise me," said O'Bryan coolly. "That was pretty straightforward."

"Well, you said to play the race card. Nobody likes a scandal."

"Indeed."

"If the bodies are still there, then we have to call for the full exhumation. This will be a fact-finding-operation, if you will."

"Well, can you get whoever does the digging thing sorted for asap? I want to be on this today."

"A team of forensics officers, I suppose. I'll try them first. I've never been involved with anything like this."

"Well start now."

"I'll call Swanvale as well, tell them to expect us today."

He nodded. "Good. Are you okay?" he asked.

"Sure, *Superintendent*, why do you ask?"

O'Bryan thought for a moment, decided to leave it at that. "As you were, DS Hosking. Can you get a minion to make me a coffee please?"

She nodded and left. He looked at the four walls and stood up decisively. He was isolated here, needed to see what was going on. The CID suite was three doors down and fifty-feet away. DCI Trevithick was in his office. DS Hosking was talking at the whiteboard with the overweight detective, DC Pengelly. Two younger detectives were looking at a screen, one bent over the desk pointing at the screen, the other sat comfortably back in his chair. They looked up but said nothing as O'Bryan walked in. They would have heard about yesterday. Half of the police in Cornwall would have heard about yesterday.

DCI Trevithick walked out from his office with DS Harris. "Good morning, *Acting* Superintendent," he said churlishly. "How would you like to tie up our criminal investigation department today? Another leisurely lunch? Some more swimming? I imagine just some crazy golf, a pasty and an ice cream and you will have ticked off your holiday list." He smiled, held up a hand. "Just a joke. Seriously, how can *my* CID team be of assistance?"

O'Bryan returned his smile, although his eyes were humourless. "Thank you DCI Trevithick. Your sarcasm is expected, although thoroughly unappreciated. But since you feel confident enough to attempt to humiliate me in front of your team, I will return the gesture. You can start by telling everybody here why you decided not to take further action when the Elmaleh family's grave was desecrated?"

For a moment O'Bryan thought the DCI was going to swing at him. Part of him hoped he would. He was ready and more than able. But the man looked crestfallen instead.

Trevithick shrugged, looked at DS Harris. "You went out to that shout, fill the *Acting* Superintendent in, will you?"

"No, I asked you. I was addressing *you*. I have seen DS Harris' report. It goes on to say that it looked like the grave had been dug-up. That the vandalism was in fact superficial. Damage to a vase and some edging stones, but the headstone was intact. It was flagged as no further action. By *you*." O'Bryan stared at Trevithick. "Care to explain?" DCI Trevithick looked flustered, but O'Bryan didn't give him the opportunity to respond. "While we're at it, and we broached this subject yesterday in case you have already forgotten, why were the sea conditions not taken into account? Flat and calm, according to the Harbourmaster's report. Not the sort of conditions to sink an inflatable vessel which was equipped with ten separate air chambers. Then there's the matters which struck me as obvious. No engine, no equipment found, not even an oar. The tide brings in all five bodies, the remains of the boat, but no oars. Interesting. Or what we detectives would call *suspicious*. But we have the biggest anomaly of all, in that the boat was purchased just three miles from this station."

"So you're saying their deaths were in fact murder?" Trevithick scoffed. "Those illegal immigrants…"

"Asylum seekers!" O'Bryan snapped. "Two doctors, both successful professionals, both trained in Europe, one of them educated at Oxford, three innocent children. Their deaths are unexplained at best. They were not commodities, unfortunate statistics. They were killed in this country, whether or not it was an accident or misadventure, there were enough anomalies to have investigated further." He looked at the rest of the team. "Who else here thought that the incident required further action?"

The detectives looked blankly at each other. There were awkward expressions all round, until DC Pengelly slowly raised his hand. "Sir, I pointed out that there were no oars, engine or fuel tanks," he said, avoiding the DCI's glare. "I just thought, well, you know? We're not near Dover, they couldn't have set out from France without an engine…"

"Good," O'Bryan said. "And why was this not added to the report?"

The officer was almost shaking, his face flushed scarlet. He was sweating profusely. O'Bryan knew the man's heart would be pumping wildly. "Sir, the DCI discounted it."

O'Bryan nodded, looked back at the officers in turn. Trevithick had turned pale. He noted that DS Hosking was supressing a smile. "Now, the man who disturbed the people digging the Elmaleh family's grave, did it not seem a coincidence that he died later that day?"

There were looks all round, a few vacant expressions. DS Hosking half raised a hand, but lowered it sheepishly. "It does, on reflection. But the death was deemed an accident and it wouldn't have come across CID's desk."

"But it did," O'Bryan corrected her.

She frowned. "But…"

"Sir," one of the men O'Bryan had not seen before today held a hand up, just halfway then dropped it back to his side. He avoided looking at Trevithick. "DC Adams, sir. I mentioned that it was a coincidence that he died the day he witnessed the event at Swanvale. But I knew John Turner. I grew up as a harbour rat, always fishing and swimming, diving off the harbour wall. I *lived* my summers at Flushing. Turner was fishing all that time. I saw him swim with his nieces and nephews a few times, taught them where to jump off the quay. He wasn't a great swimmer technically, but he was better than most fishermen."

"It was flagged up. And yes, DC Adams queried events, but it was overruled and no further action was taken." O'Bryan looked at DCI Trevithick. "Why was that?"

DCI Trevithick shook his head. "The man was seventy. He went overboard, got caught up in his lines…"

"He *was* seventy, but he was as fit as a fiddle," O'Bryan interrupted. "He dug graves, trimmed and tended the gardens of rest. He set and pulled up his lobster and crab pots most days. By hand. I suspect he was fitter than anybody in this room."

"But he couldn't swim," Trevithick protested.

"No? DC Adams told you different."

"The statement from his wife said he hadn't swum in years!"

"But that would indicate that he *could* swim, and you don't forget how to swim. It comes back pretty quickly if you fall over the side of a boat."

"I hear you weren't so familiar with swimming last night," Trevithick scoffed. "We all know you can swim. Better than those you try to save, at least…"

"One more word!" O'Bryan snapped. He stepped closer, just a pace separating the two men. "I dare you." He glanced sideways at DS Hosking. "This come from you?"

"No!" she snapped, her face flashing with anger. "Of course not!"

"Take your lover's tiff outside," Trevithick goaded. "We've got next to no budget and too many cases on our books to waste any more time on this! But it came from your other woman. My, you work fast. Is that why your wife left you? Perhaps she couldn't keep up with your womanising?"

O'Bryan clenched his fists by his side. It was all he could do to stop himself from hitting the man in front of him. He took a breath, felt the adrenalin subside a little. "I've tried with you," he said. "I was sent here to look into something, discover if there was more to it than what everyone else had taken on face value. But what I've discovered, and I know to be absolutely certain, is that you are a complete dickhead. You have a high proportion of unsolved cases, far higher than the national average. You have two ongoing murder investigations that are going nowhere, four and six years in and still no one in the frame. Now, Devon and Cornwall Constabulary have the worse murder investigation success rate in the entire country. Blame part of that on the eleven million tourists each year, blame the geographical size of the region, blame the cutbacks. But today, for the Elmaleh family's case, I blame *you* DCI Trevithick, and you alone. I have spoken to the Chief Constable at Middlemoor, and you are to go over to Bodmin today and join CID on clear-up duties until further notice. You of course have the right to speak with your police federation representative, but at this

168

stage I would advise it as career and pension suicide. Simply slide in and when I am finished here, you can come back and work with the full respect of your former team," O'Bryan paused, eyeing the people in front of him. "Or not, I suppose…"

Trevithick lunged forwards, but O'Bryan drew a large circle in the air with his right hand and swept the man's punch aside. The circle completed with his hand in front of the man's face. He drew it back in a figure of eight and his hand slid around his throat. He stepped forwards half a pace and clenched his right hand with his left. Trevithick's throat pressed against O'Bryan's right forearm and his airway was shut tight. O'Bryan looked at the rest of the team as he choked Trevithick out and the man went limp, then unconscious. He eyed each member of the team in turn, then let the man slump to the floor.

"I'm going to interview a witness," he said calmly. "See that DCI Trevithick has left the building by the time I finish." He looked at DS Hosking, who looked back at him, her eyes wide. "And get somebody onto that coffee."

21

"I didn't think you'd show."

"I seem to remember you gave me little choice."

O'Bryan looked at Sarah Penhaligan as he handed her the cup of tea. She wasn't the woman he had seen at the rented house in the leather dress and the comedy high heels. This was her. Hair as red as a summer sunrise pulled back in a ponytail, no makeup, not that he could tell at least, and wearing a thin knit pullover and a pair of faded jeans. She was pretty, but understated.

"Well, maybe after last night, things have changed," he said. "Thankyou."

"You were doing all right," she said. "You fought against the current. Sometimes you have to go with it."

"Is that just swimming or a metaphor for life?"

She sipped the tea from the paper cup and looked at him non-committedly. "It's a metaphor for survival."

"Your survival?"

She shook her head. "I'll not talk here, but I *do* want to talk."

"But you're here to talk."

"I'm here for a statement about the two men who beat you up."

O'Bryan subconsciously touched his swollen, almost black eye socket. It was sore all across his cheek. "You knew them, didn't you?"

"No."

"You're lying."

"Prove it."

"I intend to."

She shrugged. "Like I said, prove it."

"You know Pete Mitchell, don't you? He works for Charles Ogilvy on Malforth Estate, just across the water from where I'm staying." He watched her expression, there was a flicker in her eyes, nothing more. But she picked up the tea and sipped. She was buying time. "You know him, don't you, Sarah." It wasn't a question now; it was a statement of fact. "He was the one with the shotgun."

"What happens when you get to the bottom of whatever hole it is you're digging at?"

"Pardon?"

"You heard."

Sarah's accent had dropped a little further down the Cornish scale. O'Bryan continued to study her face, noticed she looked defiant, resolute. He wasn't going to hear what she didn't want to tell. Maybe it was her red hair, her emerald eyes, but he knew she could have a temper. Perhaps it was a cliché, but he had found redheads to have hidden depths you didn't always want to probe. He could see she was trying to keep calm. The cup of tea was on the table, her hands clenched together. "I'm based in London. I'll be going back and continuing my duties there."

"Exactly," she said. "And where will that leave me when you're gone?" She stood up. "I'll talk some more, but not here. I don't trust the police here."

"Certain officers?"

"What do you think?"

"Sit down, Sarah."

She glared down at him. "Don't tell me what to do. Am I under arrest?"

O'Bryan shook his head. "No, I…"

"Then open that bloody door and let me out!" she snapped. "You'll be gone from here soon, but I'll still have my shit life and have to carry on doing what I do! Now open the door and let me out!"

O'Bryan had made more than one mistake. He had tried to keep the talk unofficial and he had negated the use of a recording system. He had no other officer present and he had closed the door on a young and attractive woman and himself. She was shouting at him and it would not go unnoticed in the offices outside. He felt flushed with anguish and adrenalin, but only by his own stupidity. He got out of his chair, tried to give her a wide berth for the door, but she was on him in a flash. She prodded him in the chest, her face just inches from his own.

"You don't know anything!" she screamed at him. "All you want is to come down here from the big smoke and show us how we're not as good as you, how you get things done…" She jabbed her finger in his chest again and he caught hold of her by the arms, pushed her away to arms-length. "You're hurting me!" she shouted.

The door opened and DS Hosking stood in the doorway with DCI Trevithick. DC Pengelly hovered behind them. O'Bryan looked at them for a moment, then let go of Sarah and stepped back a pace. "It's not what it looks…" he trailed off. He'd heard it before, hadn't believed the words then, wouldn't if he were them either.

Trevithick glared as him. "Not content with assaulting me, you're hurting a witness now. What, trying to coax her into a false statement?" He stepped aside, ushered DS Hosking and DC Pengelly through. "Becky, see that the young lady is escorted to interview room three safely. Constable, escort *Acting* Superintendent O'Bryan out of here."

"It wasn't like that," said Sarah. "I just got upset, is all."

"Come with me, please," DS Hosking said impassively.

Sarah looked back at O'Bryan. Her expression was one of regret, but she wasn't making any more waves. She followed DS Hosking out into the corridor.

DCI Trevithick turned to O'Bryan. "I'll catch up with you later. I'm going to make some calls of my own. Don't go too far now. How dare you lay a finger on me in front of my team…"

"You took a swing at me," O'Bryan replied. "I could have knocked your teeth out, but I chose to subdue you instead."

"You've made a big mistake."

"You're making a bigger one. I believe there has been a premeditated and determined attempt to shut the Elmaleh case down, to make it less than it is. I have already made findings, that I will not share at this time. Not until the taint on Cornwall's CID is clear to me."

"What findings? More than the bollocks and supposition you've come up with so far, I hope."

"You'll find out when the time is right," O'Bryan stared at him coldly.

DC Pengelly placed his hand on O'Bryan's shoulder. "This way, Sir…"

"Remove your hand or you won't be able to use it for a month." O'Bryan continued to stare at DCI Trevithick. DC Pengelly released his grip and stepped back. He looked unsure, but it wasn't the man's fault. O'Bryan relented, nodded towards the open door. "Go on then, DC Pengelly, lead on…"

The detective led the way, but O'Bryan veered away from him and walked past the CID suite. He followed the corridor with the detective calling after him, "Sir! Sir, you have to come with me…"

O'Bryan stopped, waited for the man to catch up. "You made a call, Detective Constable. It was a good call. You looked at the evidence and drew a good conclusion. DCI Trevithick deemed it no further action. He did that with Adams and his personal knowledge of the fact that John Turner could indeed swim. And he took DS Harris' report concerning the damage to the grave which looked more in common with grave robbing than mindless vandalism. There's a connecting factor here, and he seems to have persuaded Sarah Penhaligan to refrain from making a complaint about the man who sexually assaulted her the night two men tied me up, held me at gunpoint and beat me up. This is bullshit policing, DC Pengelly. *Don't* become a part of it."

The young man looked unsure, but O'Bryan could see he had got through to him. "What do I…"

"You turn around and go back to your workload. DCI Trevithick wanted you to escort me out. He never mentioned detaining me. Go back to work," he said and headed for the exit.

22

Sarah Penhaligan walked out of the police station a full hour later. She exchanged words with DS Hosking at the glass doors and walked down the ramp. She looked dejected at first, but her bounce was back in her step by the time she reached her Mini Cooper in the carpark. She swung her bag onto the passenger seat and slunk down into the driver's seat and closed the door.

O'Bryan turned and ran back to his car. He had left the station and driven around Camborne's one-way system and parked up fifty-metres before the building came into view. He then made his way further forward on foot, saw that her car was still parked and waited. O'Bryan now started the Alfa and eased forward, catching a glimpse of the tiny Mini as it accelerated away. He gunned the engine and sailed on past the police station, catching up with the Mini quickly, then dropping back to let another car out of a junction. He was comfortable with the lead she had on him and the car between them gave him essential cover. She was a swift driver and when the car in front turned off, he had to speed up to maintain a visual. The road was quiet with little traffic. He hoped he was not obvious, but he knew that most people ignored their mirrors in day to day driving. She had no reason to suspect she was being followed, so he relaxed and settled in approximately three-hundred metres behind her.

After passing through woods and sweeping down a hill towards the sea, O'Bryan saw that they had reached Portreath. There was a harbour to the right of the beach and an island just offshore to the left. The beach looked idyllic. Golden sand, crashing white surf fringing the dark blue ocean. They were on the north coast now, and the scenery was dramatic. Huge cliffs hemmed the beach on three sides, and the surf crashed at the base of the cliffs and surged upwards, casting its spray and colourful mini rainbows in the sunlight. Here, the sea worried the shoreline, cast its anger upon the rocks. O'Bryan could see groups of surfers beyond the breakers, more making their way down the beach to the shoreline. He watched the Mini pull into the left and park on the newly tarmacked drive of an expensive-looking, and thoroughly modern property. Again, he saw that it was for let by Clive & Gowndry, the same company as the property Sarah had been working from in Barlooe.

O'Bryan parked the Alfa Romeo on the other side of the road. There were no lines and by the look of the vehicles with roof racks and stickers, surfers had parked here to avoid the fees in the carpark, which was clearly in view at the bottom of the road on the fenced edge of the beach. He could see Sarah sitting in her car. She was talking on her mobile phone. Moments later, a red Range Rover Sport pulled in behind her. A thin, balding man got out. He had the features of a weasel. His eyes were close together, predatory. There was something unnerving about the way he moved, like he had excess nervous energy. He walked over to the Mini and took a set of keys out of his pocket and handed them to her through her open window. They talked for less than a minute, Sarah nodding like she was receiving instructions. She got out of the car and walked to the house, disappearing down a set of steps. O'Bryan realised that the house was built on a split level. He imagined the lounge being upstairs affording the best view of the ocean.

The man got back inside the Range Rover and reversed out onto the road. O'Bryan got out of the Alfa and took out his mobile, holding it to his ear as if in conversation. He nodded, then stepped up to the window of the vehicle, made an act of putting the person on the other end of the call on hold. The man looked surprised, but stopped the vehicle nonetheless.

"Hi, sorry to trouble you," said O'Bryan. "Is this your house?"

The man seemed to weigh him up for a moment. "No," he said. "My company is handling the rental. I'm Clive Gowndry," he paused as O'Bryan held out a hand to shake. He responded, looked disappointed in O'Bryan's handshake and moved on. "I'm the managing director of Clive and Gowndry, estate agents." O'Bryan frowned at the sign. The man added, "It's just me, not a partnership. The partner thing added kudos, back when I needed it," he smiled. "I don't need that now. We're the largest letting agency in Cornwall."

"Wow," O'Bryan said like he was impressed. He hoped his acting was up to it.

"So how can I help?"

O'Bryan smiled. "I love this house. Is it likely to come up for sale?"

"I doubt it. It's up for a year-long let though." He looked O'Bryan up and down, glanced across at the Alfa Romeo. "We have plenty of other properties though. There's sure to be something in your price range."

O'Bryan figured that from the look the man had given his clothes and the ten-year old motor, he wasn't getting a year in a prime rental property overlooking the beach. He nodded and asked for a card. The man naturally had one to hand and handed it to him through the window. The glass was sliding up and the vehicle was backing out before O'Bryan had put the card in his pocket. He walked back to his car across the road and got back inside to wait. He thought about the estate agent's handshake. He had learned a lot. You could tell much, if you kept your own neutral. There were limp-wristed affairs, overly-powerful and unnecessary statements of strength, dominators who twisted the wrist to put their hand on top, and there were secret society methods, designed to welcome you to a club. O'Bryan mused over Clive Gowndry's handshake as he waited in the car.

He did not have to wait too long. The car parked up in front of him and the man studied the house for a good few minutes then took out his mobile phone and dialled. O'Bryan noticed the car was a family people carrier with children's sun blinds on the rear side windows. There were a family of stickmen in the rear windscreen. By the look of it the man had a nuclear family of a horse-riding wife and three children who enjoyed cycling, karate and tennis. He watched the man get out of the car, glance both ways and cross the road to the house.

O'Bryan got out and caught up with the man as he reached the driveway. "Sir, a word please." He held up his warrant card. "DCI O'Bryan," he said. It was easier to go with the rank that was printed on the card for all sorts of reasons. O'Bryan guided the shell-shocked man off the driveway and onto the grass verge. He could see simply from line of sight that they were out of view from Sarah inside the house. The man was shaking. O'Bryan would make it quick. "You're going into that house for sexual services, right?"

"No… I…" he stammered.

"Save it." O'Bryan looked at the man. He was in his forties and losing condition. He could see the man's wedding ring. Maybe the man liked to play the odds, got a thrill out of the event, rather than just the sex. "Where did you find out about this?"

The man hesitated. "Am I under arrest?"

"That depends."

"On what?"

"On you answering my questions," O'Bryan said curtly. "If I do arrest you, it will drag through court and your wife will find out."

"I'm just crossing the road," the man sneered. "You've got nothing on me." He went to turn around, but O'Bryan pushed him hard against the hedge. "Hey!"

"Quiet. You contacted the woman in there by phone. I'm figuring once for the appointment, then another for directions when you were close, and a third time to let her know you had arrived. Right? Don't lie, the phone records will show, no matter what you do with your phone or sim card. I'm also guessing you found out about this on the internet. Your browser history will confirm as much. Your IP address will be logged." The man looked defeated. He nodded, found it hard to maintain eye contact. "Good," O'Bryan said. "How much?"

"Two hundred."

"For what?"

"GFE."

"What?" O'Bryan asked. He'd spent the last ten years on counter-terrorism. He would guess it showed.

"Girlfriend experience," the man said. "Like the sex you had with your girlfriend before she became your wife."

"What, cinema and fish and chips?" O'Bryan laughed. "Okay, I'm guessing that's the works."

"It's everything. But it's mainly the kissing," the man explained. "Prostitutes don't normally kiss. It's sometimes difficult to get turned on without that. GFE is the *whole* package."

"Right," O'Bryan nodded. He was learning on the job. "So what website did you use?"

The man shrugged. "Just a generic search. Escorts, massage, Cornwall, GFE…"

"And she had a website?"

"Not her own, no. I went through a site called Punter Street in the end. You can enter what you're looking for, locations and description. She had photos on there. She looked nice."

O'Bryan nodded. She would have looked good. He stared at the man. For what it was worth, he felt jealous. "Look, I'm going to give you some advice. You have a family and a wife. I've seen your stickmen in the window. The Pokémon sunshades." The man looked ashen, the colour draining from him. O'Bryan guessed he had never been thinking of his kids prior to one of these assignations. "You're laying them down as chips in a game of roulette. Pretty soon, you'll bet everything precious to you on black and it's going to land on red. You get prosecuted for this sort of thing, well that's your marriage gone. That's your kids out of your life, because even if you have good access, do you think they'll want to be around the guy who threw his family in for sex with a prostitute? I'm figuring not. And it *will* come out. All sorts of shit you think you can keep covered up come out in a divorce." O'Bryan had walked the walk. His addiction to alcohol had been the entire focus in his divorce, rightly or wrongly, he hadn't been painted in the best light. "That's the personal stuff. Now your job. A criminal record will change your employee contract. Your job will likely go. Sex offences never look good on a CV either, so that's the likelihood of another job gone too. A few months without salary and the rent or mortgage for the house you're no longer living in will dry up. That's without you missing the rent on whatever bolt-hole you've managed to rent. Now your credit has gone. You'll get in debt and the spiral will continue. Are you getting the picture?"

"Yes," he nodded. He seemed to be taking it in. The man's mobile phone rang. He had been holding it lamely in his hand. He glanced at the screen. "It's her," he said.

"Answer it. Tell her you'll be there in two minutes." O'Bryan watched the man, noted the tone of his voice. He was guessing what fires of passion had burned within him as he parked the car had been doused by now.

"So what do I do?" the man asked, putting the phone into his pocket. He looked shorter somehow. Defeated.

"You take that two-hundred quid and you book a babysitter. You book a fancy restaurant, maybe even a hotel room. You stop being an idiot and spend some time with your wife. Do that once in a while, and hell, you won't think about crap like this. And you won't risk losing it all again. You might even find she's been missing the best of you as well."

The man seemed to think on this. He nodded. "Okay," he said. "Can I go?"

O'Bryan nodded and stepped up onto the driveway. He heard the man thank him, but he didn't look back. He followed the path round and stood by the solid oak door. He knocked twice, clear and loud.

He heard a bolt draw back and the handle turned. The door gave an inch, O'Bryan saw there was no security chain and he barged the door open with his shoulder. Sarah gasped and stepped back. When she looked at him, her eyes blazed.

"What the hell are you doing?"

"Your appointment had a change of heart." He stepped inside and looked at her. She was wearing a figure-hugging red dress. Her hair was down, and O'Bryan noticed blonde tresses among the red.

"What have you done?" she asked. "I need that client!"

"Client? Punter, surely."

184

He didn't see it coming, but she slapped him across the face and he recoiled. His face was still sore from the beating, now it felt raw.

"You don't understand!"

"Then tell me!" He placed a hand on his cheek, but it made no difference to the pain.

"What have you done?" she said again. She kicked off the high heels and walked off into a large lounge with an entire wall of glass looking over the bay. "Oh no, I don't believe this…"

O'Bryan followed her. "What's going on? Why won't you say who attacked me, who felt you up and dragged you out of the house?"

"For God's sake Ross! Let it go!" She flopped down on the leather sofa and cradled her head in her hands. "You've made some real trouble for me…"

"It's a couple of hundred quid," he said. "I'll square it."

"You'll square it? What if he talks? What if…"

"What?"

"Forget it."

"Tell me, Sarah."

She looked up at him. "Why do you think I work nights on the bar at the pub?"

"For extra cash," he replied.

"Extra cash, yes. Or more simply, for *cash*. If I *wanted* to do this work, actually worked the hours and could keep it, I could earn three or four-thousand a week." She wiped tears from her eyes with her fingers and palms. "I earn minimum wage, for twenty-hours a week. I could make that with one half-hour appointment. But the money I earn at the bar is for me, and I'm damned if *my* money will ever come from *this*."

"Tell me what's going on."

"Just go," she said. "You've done enough, believe me."

"Who is making you do this?" O'Bryan asked.

"What do you care?" She closed her eyes and tilted her head to the ceiling.

"Come with me," he said. He wasn't even sure what he meant, but he knew he hated seeing her like this. "I can help. I can keep you safe, help you get out of this."

"You can't *fix* me," she said, looking at him through glossy eyes, her mascara smudged. "I'm not a project. I'm a person and if you are offering to help me, you need to see it through."

"I'm a police officer," he said. "I can get you help and protection. If you are being forced into this, then you need to talk to me."

"I don't trust the police. Not down here. The people I'm involved with get away with too much for me to trust the police."

"So who are you saying is bent?"

She hesitated. "Do you mean it? You can help me?"

O'Bryan nodded. "I'm getting a picture, but it's not very clear. Hazy, to say the least. Perhaps you can help fill in the gaps?"

"I can try," she said. "But I need to know you won't leave before it's sorted out."

"I won't let you down."

She looked down at her phone. It was vibrating on silent. She looked at the screen. "It's him," she said.

"Answer it."

23

O'Bryan cursed the strength of his phone signal. He seemed to have done it hourly since he had arrived.

He had driven down into the village of Portreath, turned around when he found a turning wide enough and taken the steep hill back out. He craned his neck as he passed the house and saw that Sarah was getting into her Mini. He had promised to help, and she now seemed resolute. He was convinced she had turned her back on the sex trade.

O'Bryan missed the left turning back towards Camborne, but he saw from the vehicle's satnav map that the coast road joined the A30 and he felt the drive would go a way towards clearing his head. He kept glancing at the phone on the passenger seat, but there was still no service. He used the time to think. He wound the window down halfway and gunned the engine. The Alfa was a great car to drive through the twisting corners and he relished the exhaust note as he downshifted. He wasn't exactly speeding, but he wasn't setting a good example either. Before long, after a longish straight, where he caught a good view of the sea and St. Ives in the distance, he came to a series of bends. Some vehicles had parked up and people were crossing the road. He slowed to a crawl and peered over towards the edge of the cliff, but couldn't see anything. As he reached a layby on his left, he parked up and went to see what the other people were looking at.

The abyss before him was breath taking. A sheer, three-sided bowl that dropped to jagged rock and the surging sea below. He wasn't sure whether the people had gathered to see the sight of the waves crashing and spumes of white water, or the group of seals bobbing in the troughs just outside the breakers. Either would have been quite a sight, but the drop had been dramatic enough for O'Bryan. He walked back to his car and as he drove away, he glanced at the map on the satnav screen. It simply read: Hell's Mouth. He imagined the entire stretch of coastline had many *Hell's Mouths*, but few would be so close to the road. He crested the hill and as he drove down through the narrow, twisting road and crossed a bridge, he looked to his right and saw a lighthouse set upon a jagged rock, the waves crashing and surging to the base of the structure, the spume spraying to the top. It wasn't a sight he had ever seen before, and it made him think how static London was. Here, nature moved and changed and the sights were different every day. He imagined that in a day or two, the lighthouse would be a beacon in a millpond of glassy calm. Next week, a surging storm of grey and woeful inevitability could crash upon the shore, the sky as different as today as it was possible to be. He could smell the freshness here too. The clean saltiness of the ocean, the dampness of the woods and the pungent smell of seaweed and rotting vegetation of the creeks and rivers could all be experienced within a fifteen-minute drive from the north to south coasts of this varied and dramatic county.

After another five miles or so, he joined the A30 at Hayle and headed north. The road was a typical dual-carriageway so nobody stuck to the limit until a speed camera sign appeared and more rubber was painted onto the road. O'Bryan went with local knowledge and slowed down until he had passed the cameras on both sides. He turned off for Camborne soon after.

He parked in an empty bay, looked for the car he had seen DCI Trevithick in earlier, but it wasn't there. That didn't mean he wasn't in the station, most detectives relied heavily on pool cars. He just hoped the man had gone to Bodmin, but he didn't hold out much hope. Trevithick had been positively buoyed by the sight of seeing him in a compromising situation with Sarah Penhaligan. O'Bryan entered the code, but the door did not open. He tried again, but was met with the same locked and immobile door. He took out his mobile. The signal was good in Camborne, in most of the built up areas. He scrolled down to DS Hosking's number and dialled. It was answered on the second ring.

"Where are you?" she asked curtly. "I've been trying to call you all morning."

He frowned, he hadn't seen the missed calls. "I'm outside."

"What, outside the station?"

"Yes."

"You've got to go," she said quickly. "The DCI has been doing some digging on you. He's rather pleased with what he's found, evidently."

O'Bryan's heart skipped a beat. It was inevitable, but he'd hoped he had more time. "Where is he?"

"Out looking for you." There was a muffled pause and when she spoke again it was clearer, but he could tell she was walking quickly. "Get out of here now. Get in your car and wait for my text. I'm sending you the address, I'll meet you there in forty-five minutes."

O'Bryan did not seem to have any problems receiving her text. He typed the postcode and house name into the satnav and drove out through Camborne and back onto the A30. He wasn't on the carriageway for long and came off at North Country, taking the road towards Porthtowan. The road twisted and crested for a few miles, until it widened and dropped steeply down to a village that seemed to have been built in the seventies. There was the occasional typically Cornish stone cottage, but many of the buildings were bungalows and flats. The road threaded past a few shops, then the whole village parted on both sides to reveal the beach and ocean

191

straight ahead. The waves were steaming towards the shore in lines of five or more and breaking across the entire bay. Again, O'Bryan saw surfers heading towards the beach and could see dots behind the breakers. He figured they were surfers this time, not seals.

He looked at the satnav and realised he had to take the left-hand fork in the road. The road was narrow and climbed steeply up the cliff. To his surprise, Becky Hosking's house stood alone and imposing on the cliff. He reversed into one of two spaces and got out of the car. The view was magnificent, but as he turned his back on it and looked at the house he couldn't help but be impressed. The house was a two storey stone and glass-fronted property and from the many windows and sheer size, he figured it to have at least three bedrooms. The garden had been turned over to terraced beds and he noted that the grass around the other properties was largely thick with weeds, and he could see the sand through the storks. There was an element of reclaiming wild land, and nature was unrelenting and constant. He imagined storms roaring onshore in the depths of winter, salt spray and sand whipping up the entire valley.

The BMW Z4 sports car threaded up the narrow access road and O'Bryan could see DS Hosking clearly behind the wheel. She waved and swung the car next to O'Bryan's Alfa Romeo. The car was a convertible, and the folding metal hardtop unfolded from the boot, reached over her and eased closed, sealing silently shut. She opened the door and got out, walked up to him and smiled. "Let's talk inside," she said.

O'Bryan followed her up the steps. He noted the flush-fitting lights set into each one. The finish to the property was impeccable. He noticed things. It helped in his profession. Sometimes they mattered, sometimes they didn't. He had glanced down the side of the property as he climbed the steps. DS Hosking hadn't seen him look that way. Or maybe she had. She was a detective as well. Whether she had or not, he would know once they were inside.

The solid oak door was fitted with two locks and DS Hosking opened them both with separate keys. She swung the door open and stepped inside. O'Bryan followed.

"Coffee?" she asked.

"Please."

The flooring was solid and made from hardwood. It echoed off the stone walls. He followed her into the kitchen and watched as she hit a keypad set into the wall next to a coffee machine. He recognised it as something Italian and similar to the one he had failed to operate successfully back the Hemingway House. She took two espresso cups out of a rack next to the machine and placed them under two spouts. The machine whizzed and spat and two dark streams of liquid ran out.

"Cappuccino?" she asked.

"No, espresso will be fine," he replied.

She handed him the cup, then tipped her own shot into a larger cup and sprayed in the frothy milk. "Well, you've certainly got the DCI in a flap," she said casually. "He wants to catch up with you. Big time."

"Why," he ventured. He already knew the answer.

"Beats me," she replied.

"Really?" he said, genuinely surprised.

"Yes. He's not sharing. But he wants to find you."

"Officially?"

"Not yet," she said. "He hasn't posted a search or anything."

O'Bryan nodded. He felt a little relived, but not much. "Well, he knows where I'm staying."

"So what did you find over at Malforth Manor?" she asked. "You got into trouble swimming back, by all accounts."

"I told you I got into trouble. It accounts from nobody else." He sipped some of the thick, strong coffee. He had it down as a Java blend. "So who told DCI Trevithick?"

"Not me," she replied curtly. "Perhaps your girlfriend did."

"Sarah isn't my girlfriend. To be honest, I don't know what she is…"

"I do," she said cuttingly. "She's a whore."

"Ex-whore," he said. "As of an hour ago."

"Really? Well, we'll see about that." She took a mouthful of her cappuccino and left a little frothy milk on her top lip. She licked it off with the tip of her tongue and smiled. "So what are you… a *fixer* or something? You see a damsel in distress and play the knight in shining armour?"

O'Bryan shrugged. "I am in a position to help. I don't believe she's dyed in the wool. In fact, I know she's not. I think she will turn her back on that life forever, as long as she has some help getting out. Why wouldn't I want to help?"

"Well, we all make our beds."

"Speaking of which, you have more than enough beds here," he said. "It's a large house for one."

"I like a lot of room."

"You've got that," he smiled. "Mind if I use your bathroom?"

"No, go ahead. Top of the stairs, third door along."

O'Bryan put down the cup and made his way out into the hall and up the spiral staircase. He knew why she hadn't said left of right. The entire facing wall was tinted glass and looked out on the ocean. He went straight to the first door and saw it was an empty and unmade-up spare room. An open, empty fitted wardrobe and a double bed with a new-looking mattress. The next door opened in on a completely empty room. A fifteen by fifteen with a window looking out on the cliff behind. No curtains or blinds even. He ignored door three and opened the fourth door. The bed was made. The covers were red and there were scented candles all around and a box of matches within handy reach. A digital wireless speaker for smartphones or iPods. There was a flat-screen TV with a built-in DVD player mounted on the wall and a selection of DVD's on the dresser. He didn't have to look too closely at the covers to see they were hard-core pornography. On the bedside table were wet-wipes, tissues and an onyx bowl filled with a variety of condoms. O'Bryan opened the drawer, closed it quickly. A selection of sex toys, but he knew he would find those already. He stepped out and closed the door behind him. He opened door three, the bathroom, and pushed the flush and ran the tap. It was important to keep up pretences.

O'Bryan walked back down the stairs and out into the lounge. He looked at the view and seriously doubted anyone could ever become bored of it. He could hear her behind him. "How long have you lived here…" He didn't finish the sentence, just felt the dull thud on the back of his neck and a stab of pain run down his spine. He was aware that he was falling forwards and unable to break his fall, but was unconscious before he hit the solid wooden floor.

24

His eyes had become accustomed to the gloom. At first it had been pitch black. And then there had been bursts of orange and red. He knew he had been moving, and he knew from the smell of fumes and the sound of the engine and exhausts that he was in the boot of a car. His head had knocked against the bulkhead, and each time the vehicle braked, he was pressed into the back of the rear seats. The glow had come from the brake lights, and uncomfortable though the experience of braking was, he welcomed the dull glow of light they gave from the dark.

O'Bryan kicked and fought at first. His hands were bound tightly behind his back. He could feel the tape digging into his flesh and the adhesive tugging at the hairs on the back of his wrists. His struggle dislodged part of the trim inside the boot, exposing the rear light cluster. It didn't let in much light but what little it did, brought a welcome respite.

There was no telling how long he had been unconscious, but he would have guessed that from first waking in the darkness to the car parking up on what felt like rough ground, was no more than fifteen minutes. He had heard the door slam and then another car door opening and closing. The other car had sped away, some loose gravel hitting the car he was inside. He tried to remain calm, but his nerves were getting away from him. Was that it? Was he parked somewhere so remote that his fate was already sealed? That he would die from asphyxia, thirst or starvation? Which one of the three would kill him first? His subconscious played the odds, although he tried to put the thoughts out of his mind altogether. He thought of his daughter, but to his despair he could not picture her face. He thrust his feet out in rage and kicked more trim away. There was no extra light to be gleaned from it, but it relieved his frustration somewhat.

After what he estimated to be thirty minutes, the sound of a car approaching was clearly audible. The car manoeuvred on the gravel and the engine died. O'Bryan could hear another vehicle. There were doors opening and closing. Muffled voices, indeterminable from the confines of the boot. This second car drove away again. O'Bryan screamed for help. He was desperate and kicked out at the bulkhead, then changed to thrusting his knees against the boot lid. He changed methods again, getting greater purchase by bracing his left knee against the bulkhead and thrusting out with his right. He continued his cries for help, every breath, every ounce of energy being put into making himself heard.

There was a sharp bang on the boot lid. Then two more. A man's voice, deep, but no regional accent. "Shut up!" he shouted. "Nobody can hear you up here!" Three more bangs on the lid.

O'Bryan's heart sunk. He had already stopped banging and shouting, his heart was pounding and he fought for breath. The air was stale and felt thick and hot. He knew he was using up oxygen faster than it could get into the confines of the boot.

"I'm opening the boot," the voice said. "I have an axe. Try anything and I will stove your head in." The tone was confident. A man used to giving the orders and getting his own way.

The boot-lid clicked open and the shaft of light which poured through blinded him. He squinted, struggled to see anything at all as the lid opened more and the man stepped back cautiously. O'Bryan blinked and looked up at the man, having never felt so vulnerable in his life. He was scared, but needed to look at every angle. He needed to find a way, somehow, to avoid the inevitable. He could see Chloe's face clearly now, as if his daughter had projected herself into his mind and had given him an extra reason to live.

"Who are you?" he asked. He had to start somewhere.

"The last person you're going to see." The man stepped further back, his hands clutching the axe so tightly his knuckles had turned white.

"Did you say that to the Elmaleh family?"

"I said get out."

"To them?"

"To you, dickhead!"

"So what about them?" O'Bryan asked. He still hadn't moved.

"I said a lot."

O'Bryan looked at him, took in every detail he could. He had learned this in counter-terrorism. Every detail should be logged; all information was useful. The man was six-two and slim. O'Bryan guessed around eleven stone. He would have a stone and a half or perhaps two stone on him, and that counted if it came down to a struggle. But it didn't count for much with his hands bound behind his back.

The man was also smartly dressed. O'Bryan didn't own suits as smart as this. Not on his salary. There was a plain watch with a leather strap on the man's left wrist. The watch was extremely thin. So delicate that it looked at odds with the axe. He couldn't see from this distance, but he guessed at a Patek Philippe. O'Bryan had never seen prices on them in jewellers' windows, which had always told him they were out of his reach.

"But you killed them," O'Bryan said flatly.

The man nodded. "Now get out."

"Why did you kill them?"

The man shrugged. "Business."

"Feel good did it, to take a person's life?"

"You tell me." He smiled. "You know what it's like. You may say you don't but we all know. You fooled no one!"

O'Bryan hesitated. The comment had side-swiped him. He regained composure as best he could. "You killed a *family*. You killed a mother, a father and three young children…"

"You killed *somebody's* child," the man smiled. "But it wasn't just me."

"Who else?"

The man smirked. "No, no, no," he said quietly. "Get out of the car and kneel down."

"Make me," O'Bryan said defiantly.

The man shrugged like it was no big deal and swung the axe. He used the back edge and it came crashing down on O'Bryan's lower right leg. He screamed an agonising wail, stabs of white-hot pain shooting up his leg. He clenched his teeth, realised he had stopped breathing. The pain was excruciating and seemed all the worse for the simple fact he could not reach out and touch it, exacerbated by the tape around his wrists.

"How's that for starters?" the man sneered. He spun the axe in his hands, the blade spinning and catching the light. "Now get out, or I'll start chopping you up where you lay…"

O'Bryan kicked his legs until he got them over the edge of the boot space and dangling over the rear bumper. He struggled to sit up and the man watched him battle the angle, the boot-lid and the rise of the opening itself. He seemed bored and reached in and pulled him by his collar. He stepped back when

O'Bryan was upright. He was breathless, his leg feeling as if it were on fire, yet at the same time, numb and lifeless. He could see a car parked broadside to them. It was a new model Porsche 911 in gleaming gun-metal grey. It went well with the suit and the watch.

"Stand up and walk to the driver's door," the man said. O'Bryan turned around, finding it difficult to put weight on his leg. He realised that the car that had been his prison was his own. That made it seem all the worse somehow. But his thoughts were cast aside when he saw the view in front of him. The front wheels of the Alfa Romeo were just a few feet from the edge of a cliff every bit as sheer and dramatic-looking as Hell's Mouth. He could see the rollers breaking and hear the crash of the waves on the rocks below. "The surfers call this place Chough's Haven. They climb down with ropes, or paddle around the point to surf here. But the conditions have to be right. No good today. The wind and tide are all wrong," the man said. "So nobody will disturb us up here…"

O'Bryan had been twisting his wrists. Working at the strong tape. He was past hoping he could break free. Perhaps he could damage his skin to leave enough evidence to show that his end had been foul play. Again, Chloe's face came to him. The once cloudy memory of her giving him hope and the fact that he had more to fight for, more to live for than the meagre existence he had been living since losing everything he held dear through drink. His memory seemed to be willing a fight from him.

The man opened the driver's door as wide as it would go and stood back. "Get into the car," he said coldly.

"It won't look like an accident," O'Bryan said.

"Let me worry about that. The tide is always in here, no beach to submerge. Even at low tide there's six-feet of water at the base of the cliff. Maybe your car will never be found. Winter is coming and the surfing won't be great here. Maybe the crabs will have stripped you to the bone by spring…"

"But perhaps not. Look, my wrists are bound," O'Bryan paused. "I'm telling you, it won't look like an accident. Have you even thought this through?"

"Of course!"

"You're not the brains of the outfit, are you…" he stated sardonically. "You're the monkey. Where's the organ grinder?"

"You shut your face!"

"No gloves," said O'Bryan. "When you first drove me here, you didn't have gloves, did you," he laughed. "So there are second-person prints in and on the car. DNA also. I have an injury not conducive to the crash or fall. They will see the blunt end of that axe head imprinted on my skin and deep bruising in the muscle. It won't match anything in the cabin of the car. Seriously, who has set you up for this? Who's the organ grinder to your dumb monkey?"

The man caught hold of O'Bryan and pushed his face close to his. "I said, shut your face…"

The man didn't get to finish his sentence because O'Bryan snapped his head forwards and head-butted him on his nose. The crunch was sickening. The man recoiled backwards, but caught himself on the open door and didn't fall and nor could he move away. O'Bryan followed with another snap of his head, his forehead hitting the ruined nose again and smashing it flat. Blood and mucous left the wound in a sickly-looking clot and the man fell down onto his knees. O'Bryan checked his balance, steadied himself against the car, then thrust his knee up and under the man's chin. His head whipped up and he fell back against the door again.

Whether it was rage, or whether it was his sense of survival – threatened by his hands still being bound – but O'Bryan did not stop kicking. Nor stamping. By the time he regained control, the man was limp and motionless. O'Bryan was heaving for breath and perspiring heavily from his brow. He leaned back against the car, his legs felt like jelly and his right leg throbbed from the pain of the axe head striking him. Adrenalin was catching up with him and it was all he could do to remain upright. He took several deep breaths, so deep that his lungs could not take any more. He exhaled slowly and steadily through his mouth, then inhaled again through his nose. It had a calming, steadying effect. He did this methodically for half a dozen breaths. His heartrate lowered and the feeling of light-headedness from the rush of adrenalin subsided.

He looked down at the man on the ground. He was pretty sure he was dead. There was no movement from his chest or stomach. O'Bryan couldn't exactly give him first aid, wasn't sure he wanted to either. He looked around for the axe. It was behind the car door and just a foot from the cliff edge. The full horror of his fate lay in front of him. A vertical drop of at least three-hundred feet to the surging sea below, with jagged rocks the size of family cars breaking the water's surface. He felt the effects of vertigo as he stood on one leg and eased the axe back from the edge with his right foot. The pain was almost intolerable. When he was a safe distance from the precipice, he used his heel to drag the axe back through the seagrass and sandy earth.

Positioning the axe proved difficult, verging on the impossible and he almost abandoned the idea several times. Part of him wanted to simply walk away and find help, but another part, albeit a small but significant part of him, a part his councillor had referred to as the 'darkness' wanted more. O'Bryan knew it was there, had battled it all his life. He knew he was a fundamentally good person and wanted to help people who were unable to help themselves. But he also knew, and had become comfortable with the fact, that he could get to his ultimate goal by any means possible.

He had pressed the back edge of the axe into the ground using one foot to guide the shaft of the axe and another to sink it into the soft, sandy earth. He had then squatted carefully, painfully over the horizontal shaft and dropped down into a sitting position. It had taken three attempts, each time he had got unceremoniously back up and pressed the axe further into the soil. On his fourth attempt the axe remained firmly pressed into the earth. He shuffled backwards, got his hands in place, and started to rub the tape on the blade. As he suspected, the axe was about as sharp as a spoon. The sheer weight of the head, length of the shaft and tapering vee of the blade was what got the job done against stubborn logs. He did not have to fear cutting himself on the blade, but after what seemed like an age, friction finally got the better of the tape and combined with the pressure of his attempt to splay his arms, the bonds finally tore apart.

26

Sat at the very edge of the cliff, he watched the sea surge and froth at the bottom of Hell's Mouth. He could see the seals and seabirds bobbing on the swells behind the breakers. There was a lot of weed draping off the smooth, wet rocks below and the fronds of weed swayed hypnotically with the ebb and flow of the tide. He figured the seals enjoyed protection from people disturbing their habitat, thwarted by the inaccessibility of the steep three-sided cliffs.

There were no walkers, no sightseers parking up to look into the abyss. There was a single parked car in front of his own, and so far, he had seen no one. He decided to take the chance and stood up. He stretched casually, taking in the area in every direction. Satisfied he was alone for now, he bent down and caught hold of the handle of the axe. Another glance around, and he heaved the axe out into the air in front of him. He watched as it spun end over end and travelled a shallow arc before dropping straight down to the sea. O'Bryan saw an indistinct splash between two breakers and nothing more.

He watched for a moment longer and found himself staring at the sea, his thoughts concentrating on nothing more than the events on the cliff top less than five miles away. The man had asked him what it felt like to kill someone. And now he knew. But he had known before, and he had known what it was to live with such things.

You know what it's like. You may say you don't but we all know. You fooled no one...

Seven weeks earlier
Westminster Bridge, London

The slash on his shoulder stung like a hundred wasp stings. He could feel the blood running down his back, or maybe it was sweat. Maqsood's breath was foul, along with his body odour. O'Bryan gripped the man's wrist like it was a lifeline, which indeed it was. He had the knife in his control. If he let it go, then Maqsood would be more dangerous. And to a certain extent, the blade was plugging the wound until the SCO19 boys got here, and the paramedics would have been called already for the injured civilians, they wouldn't be too far behind.

Maqsood was grunting with the effort of resisting O'Bryan forcing him backwards, he had still been chanting his prayer, but O'Bryan had become oblivious to the noise, concentrating only on the knife and keeping him from getting control of it in the fight. Maqsood cannoned into the railings and stopped. The knife travelled deeper into O'Bryan's stomach and he rode right up against the man. He grimaced, and Maqsood grinned fleetingly, but O'Bryan snapped his head forwards and smashed his forehead into the man's nose. He wrapped his right arm around him, caught hold of the back of his head and head-butted twice more, pulling the man's head forwards to increase the force. Maqsood's eyes watered, and his nose bled as it shattered and crushed, spreading across his face. O'Bryan knew the pain the man would have felt, and keeping his grip on the man's wrist, his fingers digging into the tendons, his nails ripping the flesh, he brought his knee up into the man's groin. Maqsood let out a gasp of air, wet with mucous and blood, and O'Bryan could hear the shouted commands of the first of the armed police officers as they arrived on the scene. Maqsood pushed O'Bryan, his grip still on the handle of the dagger, and O'Bryan shoved back harder. He felt Maqsood's foot connect with his groin, and the man gripped him behind his head also. They toppled, the wind tugging at their clothing as they fell.

O'Bryan had felt the sensation before, many times, diving from ten-metre boards as a teen. Internal organs rising with the fall, a displacement that seemed to last longer than was imaginable for the distance involved. Maqsood screamed, and O'Bryan guessed it was the man's first time. The knife had come clear and O'Bryan had released his grip on the man as they fell. O'Bryan tucked and turned it into a dive worthy of just one point. It was better than the Pakistani's though, who hit the water flat on his back. The water was cold, icily so, despite being early-summer, and as O'Bryan made for the surface he could see only a few feet before the gloom became total darkness.

Maqsood had landed flat and gone shallower. He was clawing at the surface when O'Bryan came up. He was flailing wildly. The current was strong, O'Bryan could feel the drift and noticed the Houses of Parliament passing rapidly by them. He glanced upwards. The Westminster Bridge was no longer above them, it was already fifty-metres distant.

"Help me!" Maqsood blurted. His voice was wet, thick with panic and a mouthful of filthy water. "I can't swim!" he screamed, his voice cut off as he dropped below the surface, then re-emerged, mid-sentence, "…elp me!"

O'Bryan took a few strokes towards him. His stomach contorted in agony, like cramp in tired, over-worked muscles, sharp jolts of pain tearing at his senses. The water was high in salt content, and Christ knew what else. The stab wound had been both broad and deep. He could feel warmth on his skin, the blood swirling around his flesh, numbed and cold from the icy brown water of the Thames.

O'Bryan circled around Maqsood, so the man couldn't pull at him in a panic. He wrapped his right arm around him and started to kick to the south bank. He felt the man relax after a few strokes.

"Kick, you bastard!" O'Bryan shouted. "You ain't getting a free ride…"

Maqsood laughed, water hit his face and he coughed and gagged. "This is why you will lose. This is why you will always lose," he said. He coughed again, O'Bryan could tell he was spitting out some water. "I did what I did, and again, you weren't ready! Unarmed police… eunuchs protecting the masses… dickless and ineffective." Maqsood spluttered, but he had started to kick, adding some momentum to their progress. "I saw you in court. Your evidence was what got me off, you hid details and it made you look like a liar. I thank you for that, without you, I would not have won this great victory for Allah. I did what I did, killed those people, children… and still you save me from drowning! There is no victory for you, no way you will win your war on Islam. Our jihad will be total…"

O'Bryan stopped stroking with his left hand, swivelled his feet to tread water. He looked at the bridge, now one-hundred metres distant. There were officers on the bank, seventy-metres away. Someone had a life-ring and was uncoiling a length of rope. O'Bryan thought about the woman and the child he had seen, heads all but severed. The blood. So much blood, it seemed unimaginable. He glanced back at the riverbank. The man had got the rope uncoiled and was taking a throw. It fell way short, so he was frantically pulling it back in for another attempt.

O'Bryan spun Maqsood around. The man tried to grab onto him, but he smashed his fist into the Maqsood's sternum and the man wheezed and went limp in his arms. O'Bryan ducked down and pulled Maqsood with him by his belt. He kept one hand on the belt, and gripped the other around the man's neck. He powered downwards, kicking his feet and releasing some breath to counter his buoyancy and control his descent. Maqsood flailed his limbs and stared at him, panic upon his face, and from the speed and ease at which they descended, O'Bryan could tell the man had not taken a breath before going under. O'Bryan swam downwards, his face just two-feet from Maqsood's the entire time. It was darker, just ten-feet below the surface, but he could still see the panic in the man's eyes.

Despite the pain in his stomach and his shoulder, O'Bryan remained calm. In university, on the water polo team, he could hold his breath a full three minutes. He imagined he could still manage half of that, all these years later. He swam twice a week, forty lengths or so each session. He always did a few single twenty-five metre lengths underwater. He released a little more air, levelling out his ballast. Maqsood had gone from panic to realisation, to acceptance. When he took in a deep, liquid breath, his eyes bulged and he gasped like a fish on the riverbank. O'Bryan pulled him close to look him in the eyes. The water had blurred his vision, but he could see the life leaving them. When Maqsood went completely still, O'Bryan spun him over, then pushed him downwards towards the bottom of the Thames and the secrets it held. He brought his feet down on

Maqsood's back and used the corpse as a springboard to push himself towards the surface.

28

Sixty-days…

"By Christ let me make it to sixty-one…" O'Bryan muttered quietly.

He wasn't a religious man, but he did ask the Lord for occasional help. He had taken all the steps on his path to recovering, but the Alcoholics Anonymous sobriety program relied heavily upon spiritual guidance, something he had struggled with at first, but later became more relaxed with. He used his daughter as his focus and asked a higher entity for help from time to time, even if he didn't actually intend to swing from agnostic through to believer. He wasn't arrogant enough to be an atheist, just practical enough to require further proof. In times of despair, asking for a little extra help certainly couldn't hurt. In good times he gave no further thought to the matter.

He watched DCI Trevithick leave the building. He looked shabby. Overweight and untidy, a lethargic gait. He was a worried man, or should be. His career of late had more than enough discrepancies. He doubted the detective had always been this way, decisions were everything and there had to have been a watershed moment. A point where a line was crossed and the descent was made. O'Bryan had read the man's file. He knew that moment, or at least he could cross-reference with the other files he had taken from the man's computer when DS Hosking had been the last to leave the office. Or second to last.

O'Bryan got out of the car and stood calmly beside it. He closed the door sharply and DCI Trevithick looked up. Casually at first, but then he seemed to compute. He looked at the car, then at O'Bryan and his face fell. He seemed to grow taller, broaden and when he walked over, it was with a renewed vigour.

"You faked it!" he shouted. As he walked closer, he lowered his voice accordingly, but he glared nothing but anger and hatred. "Or that old bastard Anderson did…"

"You won't talk about him like that," O'Bryan said quietly.

"The old sod's dead," Trevithick paused. "You never said he was dead either."

"You never asked."

"You thought I'd see through it if I knew he was dead," he said. "Thought I'd deduce something was amiss."

"Having seen your work, I never thought you'd deduce a thing…"

Trevithick scoffed. "So who faked it?" he asked. "You or him?"

O'Bryan thought for a moment. It couldn't hurt and the trail would be as cold as Anderson's body. "He did, I guess."

"So you're not *Acting* Superintendent then?"

217

"No. Just a lowly DCI," O'Bryan said. "Like yourself."

The man looked at him coldly. "And you're not even down here officially? You don't have the authorisation?"

"No."

"I know. I checked. You're still on sick leave." Trevithick looked like he didn't know whether to laugh or cry. O'Bryan figured a little of both. "No wonder you didn't want the letter photocopied. So, what, you ran it off on a computer, copied and pasted the headed paper and forged the signatures?"

"You don't hear so well," O'Bryan smiled. "Commander Anderson provided me with the papers," he lied. "I thought they were originals."

"I bet." He looked at him, seeming to decide his next action. "I could arrest you," he said.

O'Bryan shrugged. "You could. But I'd only be out as soon as my brief took a look at the letter. It's a highly convincing forgery. And I seem to remember thinking it wasn't legitimate earlier today, since then, I've been driving around thinking what to do. A real dilemma. I've been taking in the sights, thinking it all through. Then thought I would come and see you personally," he said. "Which is why I'm here at Camborne police station, hoping to speak to you before the end of your shift." He looked at his watch. "I take it you want to leave on time?"

"Well, fuck off then," Trevithick said. "Fuck off back up country and don't come back." He turned and walked across the carpark to his vehicle.

"Trevithick!" O'Bryan called after him. "What about the exhumation? Just tell me what you found…"

DCI Trevithick turned around and looked at him for a moment. He shrugged and said, "They weren't there. You were right all along. Somebody took their bodies…"

29

O'Bryan pulled the car up onto the drive at the Hemingway House. There were two cars parked in front of him. One was Sarah's Mini Cooper and the other was a sign-written Ford Focus from a domiciliary care agency. The lights were on inside and he could see a woman in a nurse's uniform talking to Sarah through the kitchen window. He opened the door and smiled at the two women, then looked at Sarah.

"Sorted?"

She beamed a smile. "There's a place for her at Pol-an-Garrick. It's lovely and Marie here has helped me with the paperwork for funding and means-testing."

The woman nodded. "And there will be an initial payment, you say?"

"Yes," O'Bryan said. "To cover matters until the funding is in place. It will be transferred tomorrow. Six months, top tier caring. We'll advise the office tomorrow, all we need are the home's bank account and sort code."

"I have that here," she said, placing a card on the table.

Sarah was so happy; she was positively glowing. She sidled up to O'Bryan, rested her head on his shoulder, wrapped an arm around his waist. "Thank you," she said.

O'Bryan nodded, he seemed a little uncomfortable with the gesture.

"Well, if there's nothing else?"

"No, that's it," Sarah said. "I'll give you a hand."

The two women walked into the lounge and the old lady looked up at them. She had a cup of tea and a biscuit and was looking extremely confused.

"Mum, we're getting you into the car now," Sarah said slowly. It was evident her mother was hard of hearing. "Marie is going to take you to your new home at Pol-an-Garrick."

"But I liked it at The Richmond," she said. "All my friends are there. Is this your house, Sarah?"

"No, Mum," she said patiently. She had explained it before. "This is a friend's house. Meet Ross, Mum."

"Are you and Sarah courting?" the old lady said, a twinkle escaping her eye.

O'Bryan shook his head as both Sarah and Marie lifted the old woman under her arms and eased her up. "No," he said. "We're just friends."

"That's what we all used to say," she replied. She tapped her nose when she was upright. "I know how it is," she winked. She had Sarah's eyes. They were glossy and full of vigour, despite the frailty of her body.

O'Bryan smiled and nodded a goodbye as the two women helped her along and out into the kitchen.

He walked over to the window and watched the jetty on the other side of the creek. The sun was low in the sky and the creek was choppy, a cold wind blowing in from the sea. He watched the buoys bobbing, noticed that further down river there were less boats than when he had first arrived. Each day there had been less and less. He supposed that there were no boats moored this far up in the winter.

Sarah walked in, a glass of wine in her left hand, a coffee for O'Bryan in her right. "Here," she said, handing the coffee to him. "Are you alright if I have this?"

"Of course," he said. "Why wouldn't I be?" he added defensively.

"I noticed, that's all."

"Oh," he replied quietly. "Well, we all have our secrets."

"Isn't that the truth…" she said flatly.

"So, are you ready?"

"Ten minutes to fix myself up and I will be."

"No, I didn't mean that," he said. "I meant, are you *ready*?"

"Oh, I am," she said. "It's time."

30

O'Bryan showed his ticket through the open window of the Alfa Romeo and nodded at the security guard as he pointed towards a row of cars nearer the great house. He stared up at the house as he neared. It had started to rain. A misty drizzle that the Cornish called *mizzle*. It was greasy on the windscreen and he worked the wipers which seemed to make it worse. The house was lit up with spotlights pointing directly at it. Ostentatious to say the least, but perhaps they had been rigged for the event. The house was a Georgian manor, painted white with twenty windows running along both the first and second floors, and a series of large bay windows and solid oak doors on the ground floor, the centre of which was taken up by the imposing granite steps to the front entrance.

"Did you come here often," O'Bryan paused, looking at Sarah seated beside him. She was wearing a tastefully-cut red dress. It brought out the red of her hair. "You know, when…"

"Sometimes," she said. "His wife rides horses. Dressage and showing. She's quite often away with her groom at shows all over the country. Ogilvy wasn't bothered about me staying over. He didn't seem to care what the staff saw."

"Until his wife found out."

Sarah sighed. "That changed everything. Don't get me wrong, I felt for her, but he soon

223

showed his true colours. Worse than me. What he did, I wouldn't wish on a single soul."

He didn't answer. He knew how people could be. He'd spent his life hunting those who would do harm others.

O'Bryan parked up and switched off the engine. "Ready?" he asked.

"It's time," she smiled. "Thank you. I wouldn't have been strong enough for this, without you."

The gravel was thick and crunched underfoot. As they reached the highly-polished granite steps, Sarah looked nervously at O'Bryan and reached out for his hand. He took it and gave a little squeeze. At the top of the steps he saw Clive Gowndry shaking hands with arrivals and engaging in small talk. O'Bryan noticed him handing out his business cards. Obviously not one to let charity get in the way of business. Sarah's grip tightened. O'Bryan squeezed back, then released. He took the invitation out of his suit jacket. He noticed the other men were wearing tuxedos. He couldn't have cared less. He'd have his tie rolled up and in his pocket before the first plate of canapés came out from the kitchen.

He showed his invitation to a middle-aged woman in a ball gown. He'd printed his tickets off, but noticed most of the guests were just showing their smartphones. He hadn't trusted the Cornish mobile phone signal. The woman admitting the guests wore a name tag: Lucinda Ogilvy. She was what he would have described as 'horsey'. She would have been late-fifties and lived an outside life. It wouldn't have been a stretch to see why Ogilvy had had his head turned by Sarah. They stepped closer and he noticed she did not bat an eyelid when she looked at Sarah. Perhaps they had never met. Sarah hesitated, looked worried at the prospect of being this close to the woman whose husband she had slept with for over a year. Lucinda Ogilvy took their tickets and smiled at them both. "Enjoy your evening," she said with a smile and then looked past them both at the couple behind.

"I take it you never met the wife," O'Bryan said quietly.

"No."

O'Bryan caught Clive Gowndry's eye and walked over. The man had a faint recognition of him and O'Bryan could see he was trying to place his face. "This morning," O'Bryan said. "The property in Portreath…" He turned to Sarah. "It *is* Portreath, isn't it?"

She stepped out around him and smiled. "Yes, that's right."

Gowndry looked at Sarah, and it was easy to see he was lost for words. His hawk-like eyes looked her up and down with distaste.

O'Bryan held out his hand and Gowndry shook it. O'Bryan didn't release, gripped tighter. "Freemason?"

Gowndry hesitated. "No…"

"No? I would swear that's a freemason's handshake," O'Bryan paused, squeezed a little harder. "The way you've linked your finger. Like if I hooked my middle finger, we'd have a little handshake within a handshake thing going on…"

Gowndry shook his head. His weasel-like features did not hide the fact he was scared and unsure what was going on. "No, I…" he stopped and winced. "You're actually hurting me now."

"So what would I get out of being a freemason? I've always been intrigued."

"I said you're hurting me!"

O'Bryan squeezed some more. He watched the man's legs buckle and he dropped around six-inches in height. "A secret club. A mafia of the underachiever and overlooked. The mediocrity of the working and lower-middle classes, bolstered by the belief they have made it to a social elite. Am I right?" O'Bryan smiled and shook his head. "No, I couldn't join," he said. "I certainly wouldn't want to join any club who would have me as a member," he laughed. He had enough strength to double the pressure he had on Gowndry's hand. He knew the man's curled-up finger would be squashing in on itself. "You've met my date, by all accounts."

Gowndry sneered. "Who hasn't?" he managed to goad.

"It's over," O'Bryan said.

226

"We'll see about that."

O'Bryan kept up the pressure, pulled Gowndry's hand towards him. "Her mother is no longer in the home. She's away from both yours and Ogilvy's influence…"

"Did I hear my name?" Ogilvy dropped down a set of thickly carpeted stairs and stopped in his tracks when he saw Sarah. "What the bloody hell…"

O'Bryan eyed Ogilvy as he gripped with all his might and Gowndry's middle finger snapped with an audible 'crack'. He released his hand as the man dropped to his knees and howled. People were staring, but they hadn't stopped drinking the free champagne. O'Bryan extended his hand to Ogilvy.

"I didn't recognise you without my telescopic sight," Ogilvy said dryly. He stared hard at O'Bryan and accepted his hand. There was no secret finger and O'Bryan kept the pressure to about normal. Well, perhaps a little firmer.

"I didn't think you recognised what was in your sight then," O'Bryan said. "Or perhaps you did and you're just a lousy shot."

Ogilvy scoffed, looked at Sarah. "Hello, my dear. Trading down?"

She shook her head. "No, just keeping better company."

O'Bryan looked at Gowndry. The man was cradling his disjointed and broken finger and doing his best to stand. He was perspiring and his face had turned red. "You'll find some ice for that at the bar, I'd imagine…"

"So what is all this about?" Ogilvy asked incredulously. "You show up at a private gathering with my ex-lover, my wife at the door. I take it making me feel ill at ease is part of some elaborate plan or other?" He watched as Clive Gowndry walked away. He clicked his fingers at a waiter and the man walked over with a tray of champagne-filled flutes. Ogilvy took one and handed it to Sarah. She accepted it and took a sip. He took two more and handed one to O'Bryan. He watched as O'Bryan accepted it, but held it away from him, looked for somewhere to put it down. "Bottoms up," Ogilvy said, eying him closely. He smiled and looked at the waiter. "Kindly take that off my guest and go and fetch him an orange juice," he said curtly. "He obviously doesn't seem to appreciate the finer things in life…" He manged to end his sentence looking at Sarah.

O'Bryan put the glass back on the tray. He could feel the heat rising in his neck. He looked towards the staircase, noticed Pete Mitchell walking down in an ill-fitting grey suit. Mitchell smiled back at him and waited at the foot of the stairs.

"You don't *own* people," O'Bryan said, looking back at Ogilvy. "You had your fun. You had an affair and got caught."

Ogilvy shrugged. "What was the price of convenience?" he asked, looking at Sarah. "What did you get from our little dalliance?"

"You covered my mother's bills in The Richmond," she replied. "It wasn't the price of our affair. It was because of what I found one day. I went to visit my mother and she had messed herself and was sat in her own faeces and still in front of the previous night's empty dishes at eleven in the morning. She had been calling for attention for hours! I told you all of this, explained that her finances were in a state and you offered her a room in one of your homes…"

"My finest home," he interrupted.

"This was months after we started seeing each other! Some girls ask for jewellery and clothes and expensive gifts when they have affairs with married men. I never asked you for a thing! I shared this with you because I was so upset and you jumped straight in and offered to give her a place at The Richmond. After what I'd seen of the state-funded home, what was I going to do?"

Ogilvy laughed. "It's not my problem!"

"She never said it was," O'Bryan said coldly. "What *is* your problem is the enforced slavery you have kept her in since. An unwilling participant to the sex trade."

"What!" he exclaimed, then looked at them both conspiratorially as people started to look over. "I've never heard such rot!"

Mitchell walked over. "Trouble, boss?"

"None I can't handle," Ogilvy said dismissively.

"I'll wait around," he said. "Just in case…"

"We're really scared!" Sarah said, but she'd managed to make it sound like something a teen would shout in the playground.

"You should be…" Mitchell smirked. "I'll bloody-well make sure of it." O'Bryan took a step forward, but Mitchell smiled and closed the gap. "Anytime, mate…"

O'Bryan stared the man in his eyes, in the light of the great hall, he could see the man's affliction to his eye. The condition was called coloboma and the misshapen iris was clearly visible. There was no doubt this was the man who had held him at gunpoint, beaten him in Hemingway House. "It will be different if I'm not tied up and you're not pointing a shotgun at me," O'Bryan growled.

"Don't bet on it," Mitchell sneered back. "We'll just have to wait and see."

"Thank you, Pete," Ogilvy said hastily. "I'll call you if I need you."

"You'll do no such thing," O'Bryan snapped. "I'm a police officer making inquiries into an investigation…"

"Who has wantonly broken my business associate's finger in front of me," Ogilvy chided. "You could lose your job for that kind of assault."

"I've done worse…"

"Oh, we all know that, DCI O'Bryan. I've seen the news footage. You did a pretty terrible job of saving that suspected terrorist fellow." Ogilvy held up his hands and smiled. "Don't get me wrong, you should still have got the medal for drowning him…"

"He wasn't a *suspected* terrorist. He killed people, maimed others and stabbed me…" O'Bryan stared at Ogilvy, whose expression had changed suddenly. O'Bryan turned around and saw why. Lucinda Ogilvy was walking towards them, a frown upon her face. He looked at Sarah then back at Charles Ogilvy. "This should be interesting."

Ogilvy looked at them both. "Whatever this is about, I'll talk it through in my study," he paused, glancing at his watch. "Say, in half an hour?"

"Works for me," O'Bryan said. He held out an elbow and Sarah wrapped her arm into it. "Let's get a drink," he said, then smiled. "Scrap that, let's find some better company…"

They found Gowndry at the self-service bar. Most of the people were still on the champagne in the great hall and hadn't made it this far into the house. A man was leaving with two orange juices and nodded at them both as they walked in. Gowndry had his finger in a glass of ice and three-finger's worth of single malt in his other hand. He sipped it and stared at them as they approached.

"Sarah won't be doing that kind of work again," O'Bryan said. He picked up a can of Diet Coke, pulled the tab and poured it into a glass. He took a glass of white wine off a tray and handed it to Sarah. "So how does it work?" he asked. "Ogilvy buys out the old and infirm from their homes for next to no money and a place in one of his residential homes. You get the houses developed or decorated and refurbished and rented out, or sold. But either way, you have a list of vacant properties to run as pop-up brothels. You know where will be empty and where will be most convenient. Unhurried sex in luxurious, safe surroundings."

Gowndry sneered. "It's not *technically* illegal. If only one woman works there, the sex is consensual and only one punter, or client, attends, then it's not classified as a brothel. He can give money to whom he likes as a gift."

O'Bryan balled his fist, Gowndry noticed and stepped backwards. O'Bryan had him pinned between the self-service bar and the corner of the room. "So help me, I'll knock your bloody block off… It's not consensual when blackmail is being involved."

"Hey, I just provide the properties!" He looked at Sarah. "That's all I do. I get a call, I'm given some locations and I come up with the property. I meet the girl and give her the keys. I don't arrange anything else."

"What's your cut?"

He shrugged. "Twenty-five percent of the take."

"Which adds up to what?"

"I think I need to talk to my lawyer." He took out his mobile phone and dialled. "If I'm under arrest…"

The phone rang and both Clive Gowndry and Sarah looked at O'Bryan. He looked at Gowndry and slowly took the ringing phone out of his jacket pocket. He looked at the screen. It identified Clive Gowndry on the caller ID.

Gowndry hung up. He frowned and asked, "What the hell are you doing with John's phone?"

"We met earlier," O'Bryan said casually. "So he's your brief?"

Gowndry nodded. "I don't understand why you have his phone though," he said.

O'Bryan shrugged. "We met earlier. I'll be getting it back to him later," he said. He thumbed the screen and scrolled down, pressed the call button. Sarah's phone rang in her purse. He looked at her as she reached for her phone, she hesitated. "Go on, I want to see the ID." She took out the phone and showed it to him. Her ID simply read: The Bastard. "Well, well. I take it this is your fixer? Or pimp, would be a better description."

"It is," she said coldly.

O'Bryan thought about the man in the suit with the hundred-thousand pound Porsche and the watch which probably cost more. He thought about the axe in the man's hands and what he was going to do to him. Then he thought of the man's face, battered and bloodied. His body lying deathly still. "So your, *pimp*," he said to Sarah, then looked at Gowndry, "And your solicitor are the same guy?" Gowndry looked worried. Sarah just looked confused. "I don't think the Law Society would like the idea of a lawyer forcing a woman to have sex in return for simply keeping her mother in a care home. No, I think that would be frowned on very much indeed."

"He's a lawyer?" Sarah asked.

"Looks that way."

"But he worked for Ogilvy. He's the one who said my mother could continue to stay at The Richmond, but only if I did *that* for them."

"And that was your price?" Gowndry looked at her incredulously.

"No," she said. "He said that my mother may well come to harm if I didn't. That a pillow could be put over her face in the middle of the night, or an accidental overdose of painkillers might be administered if I didn't keep doing it."

Gowndry smirked. "And the money didn't hurt either," he scoffed.

"I never saw a penny," she said curtly.

Gowndry sneered. "Well, if you ever fancy a quick fifty-quid…"

He never finished the sentence. O'Bryan punched him straight in the nose with a right jab, followed it up with a left hook and a right cross. Gowndry was out cold and fell down behind the bar, wedged against the wall. There was a table nearby, O'Bryan supposed for empty glasses, and he whipped off the table cloth and draped it over Gowndry's unconscious body.

"Right, let's go and talk to Ogilvy," O'Bryan said decisively.

31

Sarah knew the way to Ogilvy's study, naturally. She led them through the great hall, where Lucinda Ogilvy was talking to small groups and the party was in full swing. It had been billed as a business networking evening and charity auction. The charities were a local children's hospice, a local woman's refuge and the Red Crescent's campaign to help people in Syria. O'Bryan struggled not to find any irony in the choices, but supposed Lucinda Ogilvy was organising this night and he had no reason to believe she was involved in anything untoward.

A wood-panelled corridor led off the far end of the great hall and the entire length was lined with paintings of the estate and various portraits of its former keepers. Ogilvy was old money and the manor had been rebuilt in the Georgian years after being ravaged by fire. Sarah was full of facts and O'Bryan guessed that when she was with Ogilvy, she had been genuinely in love. She hesitated at the door. It was a double oak door over eight-feet high.

"It's okay, I'll go in," O'Bryan said. "You wait here."

She looked a little relieved, but said, "I want to see his face. I want to see what he has to say."

"No. Let me keep it calm."

"Like you did with that rodent Clive Gowndry?"

O'Bryan shrugged. "Nevertheless, give me the chance to get through to him."

He didn't bother to knock, simply pushed the right-hand door. It moved inwards and he saw Ogilvy sat at a large curved desk some twenty-feet in front of him. The polish was high, the wood dark. O'Bryan thought it to be mahogany, but he knew for sure that it hadn't come from *Ikea*. Nor had the collection of shotguns on the wall behind him. Each one was secured with a lockable clamp through the trigger guard. There would have to have been fifty of them spread into a fan. A whole semi-circle, a half-moon of exquisitely engraved metal and highly polished walnut, barrels of blue, black, stainless steel and the brown patina of Damascus steel.

"You like?" Ogilvy turned and looked at the collection.

"They're better on the wall than pointed at somebody, I suppose."

Ogilvy chuckled. "Some of them are worth a quarter of a million, perhaps a little more. Holland and Holland and the odd Purdy mainly. English only, nothing foreign." He smiled as he turned back and looked at him. "So, DCI O'Bryan, how can I help you?"

"I think you know," he ventured.

"I know Mitchell is up to something," Ogilvy said. "But I don't know what. That rat-like creature Clive Gowndry too."

237

"Then why haven't you tried to find out?"

"I've rather blotted my copybook, so it would seem."

"Meaning?"

Ogilvy leaned back in his chair, held up his hands in a gesture of accepting a mistake. "I haven't been whiter than white in business. Some of my dealings have left me compromised, to say the least."

"How so? Start with Gowndry." O'Bryan stood a few feet from the desk. He didn't look for a chair, the stance was domineering and he wanted to keep the man off balance.

"I haven't declared my interest in Clive and Gowndry. I'm in for a huge sum of VAT and tax. We also skirted a few planning issues and bribed some of Cornwall's more susceptible planning officers and parish councillors. Not merely a bung, more like a bloody fortune."

"But that would affect Gowndry."

"When I say we…"

"Gowndry will claim he knows nothing?"

"I rather showed off at first," Ogilvy shook his head. "Bloody stupid, I know. We shared the same lawyer, he introduced us."

"John Pascoe?"

"Yes! How did you know?"

"I know things. Go on."

"I'm up to my bloody eyeballs in corruption. Gowndry knows it, so we continue to buy out the people no longer able to live on their own. I use the places in my care homes as part of their payment. Gowndry has off-set profits and bought his way into most of my residential homes."

O'Bryan nodded thoughtfully, then asked, "Is there a correlation between deaths in your homes and you buying them out? A higher percentage of residents dying who have released their equity as a care package?"

"Oh Jesus…" Ogilvy put his elbows on the desk, bowed his head into his hands. "I can check. I never thought…"

O'Bryan nodded. "What about the sex trade?"

"The what?" Ogilvy looked up, his expression one of confusion.

"You know about Sarah Penhaligan's mother, don't you?"

"Look, my wife went bloody ape-shit when she heard I had been cheating on her again. There would be no second chances, and she has the majority share in Malforth, so what could I do? I ended it, but kept Sarah's mother in The Richmond. I felt I owed her *something*." Ogilvy held his hands up again. "What's this about the sex trade?"

"I think, or rather I know, that Clive Gowndry and your solicitor, John Pascoe are running prostitutes out of vacant properties throughout Cornwall."

"What?"

"Sarah has been forced into the sex trade to keep her mother in luxury living at your care home, but it has been more than merely hinted at by Pascoe that harm would come to her mother if she did not do as she was told…"

"Oh, my poor dear…" Ogilvy shook his head, his eyes looked moist and his lips trembled slightly. "The bastards! I never knew, I swear."

"So what has Mitchell got on you?"

Ogilvy scoffed, then sighed. "I have allowed that man too much freedom. I have used him in the past as a…" he hesitated.

"An enforcer?"

"Sort of," Ogilvy sighed. "He was a strong arm in some tough times. I have had many facets to my business dealings. Mitchell was a constant companion, and I confided in him from time to time. The man just had a nasty little habit of remembering everything. I know he is with Clive Gowndry and John Pascoe. I just don't know what."

"I think I do," O'Bryan said. "Tell me, why did you take that shot at us?"

"It was Mitchell."

"But *you* had the rifle."

"I took it from him. We were looking for an injured buck. A poacher took a shot at it and left the beast injured. Blew most of its snout off. Now it can't eat or drink. Who the hell takes a head shot at a bloody deer?" O'Bryan shrugged. He had no idea, but guessed it was a no-no. "Mitchell carried my rifle on the shoulder sling. He had his shotgun with him to pop a couple of pigeons afterwards. We never found the buck. Mitchell saw you and took a shot. He was trying to scare you off. He takes his role as gamekeeper a little too seriously. He got off another before I managed to snatch the rifle off him, gave him a bollocking, for what it's worth, and came down to talk to you."

"It felt like you were warning us off."

"You were with that female detective sergeant. I've had a few dealings with her, don't like her much. No leeway. By the book and be damned with it. That's not how it should work down here. There should be some leeway, a slap on the wrist, no harm done. She's in it for promotions. Ladder climber, that one."

"What were those enquiries for?"

Ogilvy shrugged. "Farm labourers. We have a lot of Polish, and they're great workers. But we've had some Romanians and they were quite a savage bunch. They fought, fucked and stole everything they could. And they weren't strictly legal either."

"You mean illegal," O'Bryan stated.

"You're as bad as she is," Ogilvy chided. He saw the seriousness of O'Bryan's expression, then added, "Mitchell is in charge of that aspect, the casual labour. The estate owns over five-thousand acres throughout the Duchy. We grow daffodils and vegetables mainly. That requires labour and lots of it, but on a casual basis."

O'Bryan nodded. "Do you know about the smuggling cave, or tunnel near where you saw us near the creek?"

"Of course!"

"When did you lock it up?"

Ogilvy pondered. "I suppose, ten years ago. Maybe a dozen years. We had some kids discover it from over in Point Geddon and Barlooe. They turned it into a sort of den. It was innocent at first, swallows and amazons stuff, but then a year or two later it was all fags and booze, then drugs and sex... It got to the point that they were practically holding raves in there. I had it sealed and bolted because some of the parents said I was encouraging illicit behaviour. I had some workers patrol around so that they got the message."

"Well, it's been in use recently," O'Bryan said. "The hinges are well oiled, the padlocks look new to me, and there's signs of the ground being walked on."

"Mitchell has something to hide. That's why he took the shots. Nothing's going to halt someone's progress like a couple of three-oh-eight bullets at their feet." Ogilvy reached for a tumbler and the decanter of amber liquid. O'Bryan supposed it was brandy. It seemed like the drink to have in one's study. "I take it you won't be joining me?" He smiled as O'Bryan shook his head. "If I know Mitchell, it'll be alcohol and tobacco. Cigarettes without the duty. Marvellous, all I need is attention from HM Revenue and Customs. What with my aversion to VAT and taxes…"

"I'll stop you there…" O'Bryan interrupted. "I have reason to believe that Pete Mitchell has brought illegal immigrants into the country, using your smuggling cave as a place to imprison them, culminating in them being exploited in either modern-day slavery or used in the sex slave trade…"

"He wouldn't!" Ogilvy blurted. He stared at O'Bryan for a moment, then shook his head and picked up his drink. He swilled the contents down, drained them in one gulp. He screwed up his face as the liquid burned its way down. "Oh, for God's sake…"

"You know it wouldn't be a stretch of the imagination, don't you?"

He nodded, though somewhat reluctantly. "And you think Clive Gowndry and John Pascoe are involved as well?"

"It would appear so," answered O'Bryan.

Ogilvy seemed to flop in his chair, like the stuffing had been knocked out of him. "Then I'm bloody doomed," he said. "It will all come out… The police and HMRC will look into all my dealings…"

O'Bryan nodded. "Oh, they certainly will. But you deserve it. You deserve to be investigated, you deserve to be fined, to have your properties seized and go to prison for a long, long time." O'Bryan turned and walked to the door. He looked back at the man behind the desk. He was a shadow of his former self, broken. "You almost had me. I almost felt you were okay. I mean, a posh twat with a dodgy past and a certain flair for skirting the law, but okay nonetheless. But you never thought to ask who Mitchell trafficked, or how many people. You never thought to ask from where, nor what has become of them. You and Mitchell are two peas in a pod. One has money and privilege, the other has come from nowhere, but I'm sure he has accumulated a great deal from other people's misery. You both have. You, Mitchell, Gowndry and Pascoe are all one in the same. They just moved on without you, left the deadwood behind so to speak." O'Bryan opened the door and left. Ogilvy said nothing and remained motionless behind the desk, staring at the floor.

32

O'Bryan took out his iPhone and switched off the recording function. He readied it again and slipped it back into his pocket. Two for two. Both Gowndry's and Ogilvy's confessions. He suspected that neither would be permissible in a court of law, but difficult to ignore, especially depending on how the evidence was either used or leaked. He looked for Sarah on his way out. He checked the corridor and the great hall. The gathering was well underway and the sound was of chatter and clinking glasses, punctuated by hoots of laughter, some sincere, some not. He walked on, checked the self-service bar. There were people in here, but this room was quieter. Business talk, or assignations. A room where privacy had been sought away from the boisterousness of the main event. He couldn't see any sign of Sarah, and in her red dress with flowing red hair around her shoulders, she would be difficult to miss. He checked beside the bar, but noticed that Gowndry had gone. He would have come round with a headache and a little worse for wear. But they had been clean punches, bruising and a split lip. The money shot had been delivered to the point of the man's chin. A real *lights-out* punch, but no broken teeth or shattered eye sockets. He knew the man would not be making an official complaint. There was too much for the him to lose. Clive Gowndry was in as deep as he could get.

Lucinda Ogilvy was no longer taking the tickets, the night was in full swing and it looked like the great and the good were in attendance. The table was empty, except for an arrangement of gift bags which had been put out after the last guests had been admitted. O'Bryan had paid a total of four-hundred pounds for both his and Sarah's tickets, so he swiped two of the bags on the way out. He glanced inside as he walked down the steps and across the gravelled driveway. The spotlights pointed on the house gave enough ambient light for him to see by, and he saw vouchers for spa days, a selection of locally made chocolates, a voucher for a meal at a local restaurant and some sort of scented candle with a sticker of a tin mine on the base, so he guessed this was some sort of advertising loss-leader for a local candle maker. He was sure that Sarah would enjoy both bags. They reminded him of children's party bags. His wife had always had them waiting for her guests as they left Chloe's birthday parties. He smiled. In his day it had been a slice of cake and a balloon if you were lucky.

When he reached his car he opened the boot and put the two bags into the cubby, then took out the torch and a pair of heavy duty bolt-croppers that had set him back eighty-pounds from a local hardware and home store chain. Among other things, he had bought a sixteen-ounce claw hammer as well. He wasn't a practical man, in that he lived in a rented apartment and seldom needed to do DIY, but he figured he knew the fundamentals to getting those wrought iron gates open.

O'Bryan set out across the lawn to the side of the house, switched on the beam of the torch and shone it out across the rear lawns. He saw the ground slope down beyond and saw lights in the distance, which he took to be those of Point Geddon. Downhill was the right direction, so he struck out, keeping the beam on its lowest setting to avoid being too conspicuous. The torch was an internet special he had owned for several years, a SWAT/special forces model that claimed to be the most powerful hand-held model on the market. Whether that was true or not, he knew he hadn't seen many brighter.

A barrier of stock fencing separated the lawns from the open field. It was a three-rung iron fence around five-feet high and designed to keep the deer or farm animals off the two-tone striped lawn. He climbed over and dropped lightly onto the ground. He instantly felt the unevenness of the ground underfoot, the grass was longer as well. The terrain became rougher and steeper, and he started to slip on early dew forming on the grass, his shoes were more suited to bars and great halls than to rambling. He turned the light setting up and twisted the aperture to get a narrower, but more concentrated beam. The light shone powerfully out to three-hundred metres and on the edge of that lay the woodland he could see from the other side of the creek at Barlooe.

O'Bryan reached the fringe of the woods and switched off the torch. He remained still for a good five minutes, taking in his surroundings and listening for the night sounds. His ears became more accustomed, as did his eyes, but he would need the torch again in a moment and that would render his night vision useless once more. He could pick out the sound of early fallen leaves rustling on the ground, the noise of small rodents or perhaps a fox breaking through the undergrowth. The occasional screeches, he put down to owls or foxes, he wasn't sure which. But he did know that in the countryside at night, there was always sounds of the hunters and the hunted. The food chain in constant motion.

When he switched the torch on again, he used the low-power setting and widened the beam. He also kept it low, searching the ground in front of him for the huge granite boulders that would tell him he was near. The woods looked different at night, and from this approach, he wasn't sure he was on track. He could see lights across the river, this time he figured, or at least hoped, it was Barlooe. This meant he was also nearing the other end of the woods. He swept the torch in wider arcs, switched up the power and closed the width of the beam down. He caught sight of the first granite boulder, the size of a small hatchback, and looked down for the trail. After a few minutes he was on it and he turned around and headed back up hill, following the trail around on a loose parallel with the creek. He made his way through the boulders, feeling a little uneasy at being hemmed in, and thoroughly relieved when he came out into the opening and saw the entrance to the cave.

He played the light on the gates, took advantage of illuminating the entire mouth of the cave, but noticed it veered sharply to the left. He used the bolt-croppers to snap the hasp of the padlock, surprised at how easy it had been. The bolt-croppers were pneumatic, giving tension a hundred times what O'Bryan could have mustered alone. He threaded the chain through the bars and let them drop to the dry earth. There was no needed for the hammer, which he had tucked into his waistband, but he did not know whether he would need the bolt-croppers again, so kept them with him as he set off down the tunnel.

33

O'Bryan could hear them before he saw them. There was the sound of muffled voices and crying. But it was more than that. There was an air of misery. He couldn't think what it was, but as he rounded another bend in the tunnel, which had been gradually tapering smaller in overall dimension, he could *feel* the depression in the atmosphere.

The walls of the tunnel were a mixture of solid rock with pick-marks and drill holes where dynamite or black powder charges would once have been used to cut through the rock. In places the tunnel was boarded with rotten-looking planks. Sure enough, in these areas, a fine dust of rock debris and dried soil rained between the planks lining the ceiling. Just a fine and occasional sprinkling, like shaking icing sugar over a cake. O'Bryan looked at the ceiling ominously. Ahead of him the roof had been haphazardly propped with four-by-four posts. These looked more like rotten wood than freshly milled timber. This section of the tunnel was some two-feet lower than the previous section and looked to have sunk over time. At just over six-feet tall, he came close to scraping his head on the rafters.

He played the beam across the walls and ceiling, hesitated when he saw the build-up of debris on the floor, but the voices spurred him onwards. He could hear the suffering, the fear, the uncertainty. He was no fan of enclosed spaces, had suffered and panicked in the boot of his car, but he needed to keep moving forwards.

O'Bryan spread the beam of the torch so that it illuminated the entire tunnel in front and to each side of him. The light was clear and blue-white. It turned the tunnel into daylight, but when he glanced over his shoulder, the tunnel was a black hole of total darkness. He decided right there and then that he would not add caving to his bucket list of activities. He could hear more voices now, and then, as he rounded the next bend, he could see movement ahead. The voices ceased and there was a sense of panic in the air. Hushed tones, quickly spoken sentences which sounded rushed and reciprocated. Another few paces and the light picked out bars on both sides of the tunnel where recesses had been dug or blasted out of the rock. These would have been stores for rum and tobacco and other goods brought in to avoid the customs officers over two-hundred years ago. A time when Malforth Manor would have been more than just a businessman's residence, but the centre of commerce and employment to the surrounding villages. This cave and stores would have either been constructed right under the Lord of the Manor's nose without his knowledge, by the very workers he employed, or was perhaps the reason for the manor owner's increasing wealth. A secret venture to keep the locals onside and in cheap alcohol and tobacco.

O'Bryan would hazard a guess that this storage cavern was indeed directly under the manor house itself. In which case, there was most likely a route into the manor, if it hadn't been sealed at some point over the years. Otherwise, there seemed little point in excavating so far.

O'Bryan shone the torch around him. There was no bounty in these dugouts. Not unless you counted humans as commodity. He lowered the torch from the blinking faces and switched to the lowest power setting. Three women, O'Bryan guessed to be anywhere from their late-teens to their early-twenties, stood at the bars to the cell on his right. He looked at the cell to his left. A man and a woman stood huddled together. They were attempting to shield a child of around nine or ten. O'Bryan couldn't see for sure, but he'd bet anything that it was a little girl. The same little girl who had lost her teddy bear three nights earlier.

"I'm here to help," he said quietly, slowly. "Does anybody speak English?"

The man nodded. "Little Engleesh…" he replied even more slowly. "I am Abdul…"

"I speak English. Who are you?" a voice behind echoed out confidently from the other cell.

O'Bryan turned around, saw one of the young women standing slightly further forward than the other two. He raised the torch, not intrusively, just enough to highlight her features. He could see dried blood on her face, her clothes filthy and ripped. There was an overwhelming fetid smell, an overpowering stench of both sweat and urine and faeces. It reminded O'Bryan of a trip he once had with Chloe to the zoo on a hot day. The domestic farmyard petting enclosure of goats in particular. He tried not to wrinkle his nose. He could see that the women had used a corner of their cell as a toilet. Near the bars, on the other side of the cell, cases of bottled water and an outer box of ready to eat camping/trekking meals in foil bags had been broken into, empty packets lay strewn next to the box. There were candles burning, but he hadn't noticed them at first due to the power of his torch. It was a medieval prison. Horrifyingly basic and would have been terrifying in the silent darkness of the tunnel.

"I am a policeman, a detective. I am a senior ranking officer," he said reassuringly. "My name is Ross O'Bryan. You can call all me Ross…"

"I'll call you Mohammed, Buddha or Jesus Christ almighty if you get us the hell out of here…" she said sharply. Her accent was middle-east meets Disney and she had a spark in her eye and a look of defiance on her face. She looked at the bolt-croppers in his hand. "Are you going to use those, or what?"

O'Bryan snapped to and searched for the padlock on the chain securing the cell bars. He put the handle of the torch in his mouth and used both hands to operate the bolt-croppers. This padlock was stronger than the one securing the entrance and O'Bryan had to take several attempts, but eventually it pinged off and the chain separated and the woman stepped forwards together and grabbed the bars. O'Bryan pulled and they pushed and the bars opened. Two of the women rushed across the tunnel and flung themselves at the bars of the other cell. There were kisses and hugging, as best they could and the woman who had done the talking hugged O'Bryan in a way he'd never felt before. A total and complete show of gratitude with a sincerity he was barely able to comprehend. She let go and joined the others, who were by now looking expectantly at him to get the padlock off. He wasted no more time, worked on the bolt and had it cut cleanly within a minute. The man pushed the door out and hugged the three young women, his eyes closed as he savoured ever particle of them, as if every second of the moment was regaining an hour stolen from him.

The man hugged O'Bryan and he dropped the bolt-croppers, taken by surprise and shaken at the power of the hug. He tapped the man on the back and the man released him, his wife was already in an embrace with her four daughters.

"Thank you, thank you," the man said.

O'Bryan was about to tell him it was alright, but the sudden illumination of the cavern startled him, and everyone else. The torch was bright, but the complete white light from the half-dozen one-hundred watt bulbs overhead was incomparable. He looked around him, noted that the cavern was indeed the end of the line. The rest of the tunnel was sealed with concrete blocks and mortar. They had been cut neatly into the curvature of the tunnel walls. He watched the tunnel, a sense of foreboding and indecision upon him all at once.

Clive Gowndry rounded the bend. He carried a shotgun. Ornate and shining in the bright light. O'Bryan wondered if Ogilvy's display fan of shotguns on the wall had a missing space. As the man neared he could see he had bound his middle finger to his ring finger with a makeshift bandage of what looked like a strip of linen napkin. It made the way he held the weapon look somewhat awkward, but his trigger finger was unaffected and wrapped around the forward trigger.

"Oh, isn't that touching…" he said, smiling. "A family reunion. Well, it won't last long. There are plans for this lot."

O'Bryan stared at him as he approached. He shook his head. "Like the others?"

"Hopefully not," he said. "They were quite a handful, the *Elmaleh's*, or whatever the hell they were called…"

"Qasim, a forty-five-year-old doctor. Yara also a doctor, thirty-nine," O'Bryan paused. "Amira, aged Twelve, Fatima aged Eleven and Mohammed, aged ten…" he spat at him. "And you killed them. You could at least remember their names…"

Gowndry shook his head. "I didn't kill anyone… That was Pascoe and Mitchell. But the trouble was, I don't think we softened them up enough before putting them to work," he added.

"Meaning? Is this what this is about?" he asked, waving a hand towards the cell. "Dehumanising them? Making them want more and appreciating it when they got it?"

"Sort of," Gowndry smiled. "These girls will be pleased for a hot meal and a shower and clean clothes. Having to fuck a dozen different men a day won't seem such a hardship when they know how tough things can be."

O'Bryan shook his head. "You are all idiots. I don't know about these people, but the Elmaleh family endured years of hardship in Syria. Little food, no clean water, hardly any medical attention. No heating in the harsh winters and no respite in the hot, dusty summers. Then they set out to trek across Turkey and Europe to get here. Month upon month on the trail, roads and in the back of lorries. They only *knew* hardship. That's why you couldn't break them down."

"No, they were a handful alright. But we've learned. The woman was a good fuck, she got the message. She seemed to catch on to what was best for her family. But the husband…" he shrugged. "We just couldn't get through to him."

"And…" O'Bryan wasn't sure he wanted the answer, but he asked anyway. It was the detective in him. "…the children?"

Gowndry shrugged. "We had plenty of bidders. A bit of a ring going on. There's plenty of people who want what the heart desires… But you've got to keep them in line. The punters, that is. They tend to talk, invite friends in on it. Well, we closed it all down to re-evaluate how best to go forward. That Syrian family were past their fuck-by-date anyhow…"

"So you drowned them?" O'Bryan spat.

He shrugged. "Mitchell did it. Easy enough. A noose on a pole. Take them down a few feet and wait. They soon stop their struggling…" He smiled. "Mind you, they didn't much like having to watch…"

"Bastards!" the woman who had done the talking screamed. She started to translate hurriedly to the rest of her family. The man and his wife looked horrified, pulled their off-spring closer.

"Yeah, well," Gowndry grinned. "At least you know what's coming if you don't play along." He walked a few feet closer, aimed the shotgun at the group. "And that goes for all you camel-fuckers!"

O'Bryan shook his head. "You thought the DNA from all of the people who abused them sexually would be lost in the seawater, didn't you?"

Gowndry sneered. "But it wouldn't be. Not for sure. Hundreds of mineshafts to lose them down, never see them again, and Mitchell opted for drowning them. He and John Pascoe thought making them look like asylum-seekers who capsized and drowned would work better. But Pascoe's police contact said that the DNA would hold up to an autopsy. Everyone sweated for a while, but they ended up buried in Swanvale without a post-mortem. We could thank the local Muslim community for that."

"But you thought you'd get them dug up and disposed of in case an exhumation and autopsy were ever sought at a later date?" O'Bryan stared at Gowndry. "Down that mineshaft you mentioned," he paused. "But he was seen, Mitchell that is, and that's when he drowned John Turner in the same manner."

"Shame, that one," Gowndry paused. "Mitchell knew him for years. Not a bad bloke, apparently."

O'Bryan still held the torch in his right hand, down by his side. He had been working the aperture carefully in his hand, tightening the beam. The cavern was well lit, but the tactical torch was equipped with a strobe, emitting twice the light of the beam, around a million candle-power and flashing ten times a second. Gowndry was six-feet away, but the shotgun looked steady in his hands. He imagined the man taking a peg at the pheasant drive and blasting eighty of the poor birds from the sky during a brandy-fuelled day with Ogilvy and their business associates. He had no reason to believe the man was anything but expert with the weapon.

"Right," Gowndry said decisively. "Get back in the cells." He looked at O'Bryan and smiled. "You too. If I were you, I'd pick the one with the younger women. One of those camel-fuckers might let you do her. If you can stand the smell, that is…"

The woman who had done the talking screeched and bolted forwards. Gowndry swung the shotgun at the same time as O'Bryan pressed the strobe button and the light disco-balled in Gowndry's eyes. He squinted, held a hand to his eyes and swung the weapon one handed. The noise of the shotgun blast was deafening in the confines of the cavern. There were simultaneous screams from the women and the husband went down. He had been skimmed by a few pellets, but those pellets had been point blank and his shoulder had turned crimson. O'Bryan grabbed the barrel with his left hand and felt the searing heat in his palm. He turned to the family and screamed for them to run. They didn't need telling twice, and they pulled their father to his feet, the mother swept up the youngest daughter and they were on their feet like greyhounds out of the gate.

Gowndry kicked out, but it was weak and he was off-balance. O'Bryan kicked back and drove the ball of his foot into the man's gut. He fell backwards, but kept hold of the shotgun, trying desperately to bring it around onto O'Bryan. He was determined, knew he was out of options and this was the last fight he'd have. O'Bryan knew it too. But he'd been in this position before, and he knew how far he could go. He threw the torch into Gowndry's face and the man screamed as it smashed into his eye. It was enough for him to release his grip on the shotgun, and it dropped with a clatter onto the ground, O'Bryan letting go of his grip on the barrels to keep a hold on his opponent. Gowndry punched and flailed, but he was not a strong man. O'Bryan caught hold of him, positioned him well, then pounded him in his already bruised face. He went down hard, a repeat of the bar, but he landed right next to the shotgun and went for it. O'Bryan calculated the distance, but he knew he'd never make it and was already running. He swept up the torch, which was still strobing and reached the end of the cavern as the shotgun blast echoed out. He didn't feel its blast, but he heard the pellets as they clattered and ricocheted off the rock walls. He could hear the man opening the breach and reloading the barrels behind him. The tunnel was long and before the next corner, Gowndry would hit him for sure. He grabbed the brand new claw hammer out from his waistband, and as he raced past the low section of ceiling, he smashed the hammer against the first of the four by four post. It rocked out and debris dropped from the ceiling. O'Bryan hit the next one, and the next. He could hear the posts clattering on the rock floor behind him, the sound of twenty-pounds of dirt hitting the ground each time. Without losing momentum, he knocked out the last post and the sound behind him was deafening. The roof of the tunnel dropped with hundreds of tonnes of rock and soil falling all at once. The lights running down the tunnel went off and turned O'Bryan's world into darkness, interspersed with the strobing of blue-white light. He was lifted off his feet by a great wind, the force of the rock-fall behind him, and it carried him a clear twenty-feet down into the darkness. He landed in a heap, his face in the dirt. He had dropped the torch, but it was impossible to lose. When he reached it, he switched off the strobe and widened the beam. The cave was entirely blocked with earth and rocks, some as large as household appliances, several tonnes in weight. He heard a sound and turned around sharply. It was the young woman who had done the talking.

"Are you okay?" she asked tentatively.

"I think so," he replied. "Where are your family?"

She shrugged. "I thought I would come back to help you," she said. "You helped us out of there… It was the least I could do."

34

O'Bryan had noticed the strobing of the blue lights, recognised the play of illumination off the walls of the building from countless crime scenes nearing twenty-years of service. He didn't know if the family had noticed. They were huddled tightly and talking in their own language. O'Bryan knew they were safe now, and had relayed this to the young woman. She had spoken to the rest of her family, but the look on their faces told him they were far from relieved.

There were three police vehicles and an ambulance. All had their blue lights operating on top. O'Bryan surveyed the scene, watched as the uniformed officers bunched the guests into a sort of holding area, while plain clothed detectives prepared clipboards for interviewing. O'Bryan frowned, but walked on with the family behind him. He saw DS Hosking and she hurried over.

"Jesus! What happened to you?" she asked. She looked at the bedraggled family and frowned at him. "Who are these people?" O'Bryan stared at her, but she raised her eyebrows in annoyance. "I'm sorry about yesterday, you saw my note, right?"

"What note?" He thought about the house, the room for clients, the hit on the back of his head, the boot of the car, the clifftop, the fight… "What are you talking about?"

"I got an urgent call," she said. "You were upstairs in the loo, I felt a little embarrassed at calling up to you, to speak to you through the door… I left a note on the kitchen table along with your coffee. Trevithick told me about your letter. What the hell were you thinking? You couldn't possibly have hoped to get away with it, acting unofficially. I didn't let on to where I'd seen you…"

"And where did you see me?"

She frowned, reached out and touched his shoulder tenderly. "Are you okay, Ross?"   "Of course," he said. "Where were we? Whose house was that? Yours?"

"No!" she replied hostilely. "I never said it was my house. It was a place in one of our investigations. I borrowed the keys, that's all. I wanted somewhere safe to talk. Hey, don't mention it, okay? I'll get into serious trouble." O'Bryan nodded and she said, "Look, we'll talk later. I have work to do."

"What's happened?"

"Charles Ogilvy," she said. "He turned a shotgun on himself in the middle of his charity gala."

"Where?"

"In his study," she said. "His wife discovered the body. She went looking for him. Seems an ex-lover of his was here tonight, bold as brass. She thought he was up to his old tricks and thought she'd catch him out. Then she found him…" She turned and started back towards the house.

He called out, "Do you know a man called John Pascoe?"

She stopped and looked back, frowning. "Lawyer. Slimy bloke." She nodded. "Yeah, our paths have crossed. He's a lawyer who turns a blind eye to stuff. His family are well respected, but they're wealthy. They didn't get that way by being nice."

"How so?"

"They own property, hotels and holiday lets. They get the planning they need and don't pay all the VAT or tax they should. Keep their staff on either zero hour contracts or training schemes that have them working illegal hours for half the minimum wage, or so I hear," she paused. "Big in the freemasons too. Funny handshakes and back-scratching. Well, they all are, aren't they?"

"Who?"

"The ones who get on down here. Those, and the ones who *want* to get on." She turned and walked back to the steps, jogged up them and disappeared inside.

O'Bryan waved at a uniformed officer, beckoning the man to come over. He did so, a little begrudgingly. O'Bryan explained what had happened, that the family had been imprisoned. He asked if he could get them some water first, then contact a senior officer. He wanted to keep it out of the hands of CID for a moment, see them entered into the system before he did what he planned next. He watched the officer walk up the steps to the house. It looked like he spoke to a waiter hovering at the top of the steps and he too walked inside. Less than a minute later, DCI Trevithick came out and stood at the top of the steps. He surveyed the area, then made his way down the steps and walked towards them. O'Bryan groaned inwardly. He backed away from the family, took out his iPhone and took a picture of all of them, huddled in their group. He thumbed the screen, then looked at Trevithick as he drew near. When he looked up DS Chris Harris was approaching from another direction. The light shone off his red hair and it made his greying beard appear whiter. He looked like Santa Clause for a moment, and the sight was surreal.

"What are you doing?" the DCI asked incredulously.

"I've just taken a picture of these people, and emailed it, along with a short report, to Devon and Cornwall HQ in Exeter. I have also uploaded it to the internal server at Scotland Yard."

"You don't trust me?"

"I don't trust anyone I meet down here," O'Bryan paused, eyed DS Harris for a moment. "These people have just become public knowledge. They have entered the system. I'm handing them over to you now, DS Harris."

"Where did you find them?" Harris asked.

"They were being held in cells built in an old smuggling tunnel on the creek side of the estate." O'Bryan watched the uniformed officer return with two waiters. One carried glasses of water and orange juice on a tray, the other carried a tray with a large selection of canapés arranged on tiny plates. It looked comical, given their state of appearance, but they did not waste time tucking in. O'Bryan said, "There was a cave-in. A section of the roof of the tunnel collapsed. Lucky timing, I guess."

DS Harris nodded towards the family. "So what's their story?"

"Refugees. Syrian I'd bet," O'Bryan paused, took his iPhone back out of his pocket. "I've got Charles Ogilvy's insight into what Pete Mitchell, Clive Gowndry and John Pascoe were up to…"

"Pascoe?" Trevithick asked. "The solicitor?"

"The same."

"Are you sure?" DS Harris asked. He looked at Trevithick, then back to O'Bryan. "There's all sorts of ramifications if that's the case…"

Trevithick moved it on. He looked like he was pressed for time and the Syrian family was another hassle he didn't need. "What were they up to?"

"I've got Gowndry's confession on here too."

"Give it to me."

"No," O'Bryan said. "When I get a better signal or onto some Wi-Fi, I'll upload it. Same as before. Exeter and Scotland Yard first."

"I could take it. It's evidence."

"You could try. I wouldn't recommend it."

Trevithick shook his head. "You think you're a real hot shit, don't you?" He shrugged. "Alright, what is Gowndry's confession. The salient facts, I've got a shit storm here."

"What's going on?" O'Bryan asked.

"You first."

O'Bryan shrugged. "Gowndry, Mitchell and Pascoe ran a sex ring together. From what I gather it ran through from straight to gay to paedophilia. But the straight aspect would still have been nothing more than rape. I don't even know how to begin classifying the rest of it," O'Bryan nodded towards the family, now enjoying smoked salmon and caviar on blinis. "These people were lucky; from what I gather. They were brought in by boat three nights ago. The night I was assaulted and you did nothing about it…" Trevithick seemed to be taking it on board. He nodded, remained silent. "Mitchell and Pascoe saw me watching them." O'Bryan looked towards the house and the gathering of guests. "So your turn. What's happening here?"

Trevithick stared at him. "Charles Ogilvy is dead."

"He killed himself?"

267

"No. Why would he?"

"Listen to the recording later."

"Well, he didn't kill himself. But he was shot with one of his own shotguns. Know anything about that?"

"You suspect me?"

"Well you turned up here tonight with his mistress in tow. And you both headed towards his study. It's not a stretch of the imagination."

O'Bryan laughed. "Not for your limited imagination, no."

"Meaning?" he snapped.

"Gowndry turned up in the cave with a shotgun. Ornate and expensive, by the look of it."

"And?"

"And he held us at gunpoint. We all escaped, I fought with him and managed to get away. The last I know of him, he was shooting at me and missed. He hit a strut, the roof caved in and he was under about ten tonnes of rock and earth."

"Shit! He's still in there?"

"He isn't going anywhere in a hurry."

Trevithick turned and took out his mobile phone and started to dial as he walked away towards the house. It was turning into a busy night for him.

O'Bryan looked at DS Chris Harris. "Right, now he's gone, I want to talk to you."

The detective nodded. "Okay…"

"Mitchell and Pascoe dug up the Elmaleh family because somebody convinced them that DNA would be an issue if they were exhumed and a proper autopsy was ever sought. That somebody was in the police."

"You suspect the DCI?"

"You called for further action in the investigation. It was denied by Trevithick. I trust you." He opened up his iPhone and thumbed down to his contacts. "What's your email?" Harris told him and O'Bryan typed it in. "I'm sending you the recordings of both Ogilvy and Gowndry, both made tonight. You need to get a search out for Pete Mitchell too. He's a priority and with a fishing boat, he has the means to get away, head in any direction and stay off the radar."

"I'll get on it." He looked at the family, now eating what looked like soft-poached quail's egg wrapped in pancetta. "I'll call social services right now and get them accommodation for the night. They look in pretty rough shape. They'll get clean clothes and a shower."

"They're crucial witnesses. They will identify Pete Mitchell and John Pascoe as their abductors."

"John Pascoe has been listed as a missing person. It's early, but he had appointments he didn't keep and it's out of character."

O'Bryan thought back to the clifftop, the axe, his battered body on the ground... "Maybe he caught wind of all this and has taken off."

"Most likely, by the sounds of it," he said. "I'll get the ball rolling here," he said and turned towards the family.

O'Bryan made his way towards the house. He needed to find Sarah and tell her what had transpired. But most of all, he wanted to warn her that the link left in the chain, Pete Mitchell, was on the run and had nothing to lose.

35

Day one...

O'Bryan awoke, ripped from his stupor by the incessant banging. Metal on metal, absorbed and echoed by wood. Heavy oak, but even that seemed to be shaking within the frame.

He should have tipped Anderson's cognac down the sink when he arrived, should have washed it down the drain with the wine and the European beer. But he'd washed the filthy liquid down his own throat instead. He had kidded himself that he could stop at one, but the devil on his shoulder dug in his claws and accepted another. And then the deal was done, he'd signed up again and drank the place dry.

He could have coped without the drink, had he not continued to recount the last moments of the Elmaleh family. The image of them scared and knowing their fate, watching their loved ones taken one by one and drowned in such a cold and proficient fashion. Who had been first? Who had been the lucky one? Who had endured the torturous scene for the duration? Who had watched the other four members taken one by one and pushed under kicking and screaming, pulled out lifeless and still? O'Bryan thought of them, used and abused, terrified and aware at the end, knowing their time had come, that they would never gaze upon their family again or take in another day. Something so casual about the way Clive

Gowndry had regaled at the facts. Those people had been nothing more than a commodity in a market almost too sick to imagine, yet alone witness. The family that O'Bryan saved from the cave would have suffered a similar fate, because as much as they would try to break them, human spirit has untold resolves and he could see it in their eyes that they would have kept fighting. How long before they too would have been drowned out at sea? Or thrown down that ominous mineshaft? O'Bryan could see the futility in life. There wasn't always someone who could help. There were countless people out there suffering even worse fates and meeting similar ends. The thoughts of this, over and over throughout the night had made him reach for a bottle. And then another. Now came the regret. Now came the knowledge the agony of over sixty days of staying dry had been in vain. That he had broken over sixty promises to himself, but ultimately he had broken the promise to Chloe. She would never know, but he would know every second of every day. Today was the first day. And today would be the hardest day of all.

The banging hadn't stopped. He had double-locked and bolted every door, feeling vulnerable that Pete Mitchell was still at large. He had uploaded the recordings to DS Harris and to Middlemoor, the headquarters of the Devon and Cornwall police in Exeter. He had also sent the file to the internal server at his office at Scotland Yard. He had sent the photographs of the family to each address as well. This family, whoever they were, were now in the system and accounted for. He could do no more for them.

He swung his legs off the sofa and stood up unsteadily. He had slept in his clothes. Now the shirt and trousers looked creased and twisted. He straightened them out the best he could and headed towards the front door. The banging was both loud and impatient. He pulled back the bolt and turned the key. He opened the door inwards and blinked at the light.

"Took your time," DCI Trevithick said curtly.

O'Bryan looked at him, but said nothing. He looked at DS Hosking standing beside him. His mouth felt like wool. He had no saliva and he knew he looked a state. "What's wrong?"

"Where were you between ten o'clock last-night and five this morning?" Trevithick asked accusingly.

"Why?"

"Answer the question."

"Am I under arrest?"

"No."

"Then stick your question."

"You're not under arrest, yet," Trevithick paused. "But that can soon change."

"Do I need a lawyer?" he asked, then looked at DS Hosking and said, "Can you recommend one?"

She frowned, shook her head. "It would be easier if you could just answer the question."

"No doubt. Is this about Mitchell? Have you found him?"

"We've found a body," Trevithick said. "Get yourself tidied up and come with us. I can make it official, if you'd prefer. Even get the cuffs out."

O'Bryan hesitated, but he decided not to taunt the man any longer. He wanted answers to his questions too, and he wasn't getting them on the doorstep trading insults.

They gave him five-minutes to wash and change. He took closer to fifteen. When he came back downstairs, DS Hosking was in the kitchen and had made coffee. She had tidied up and got rid of the empty bottles too. She looked at him knowingly. He took the coffee and thanked her. He was past embarrassed. Embarrassed was sixty-one days ago when he had woken up in his own piss and vomit. He hadn't known where he was. Enough had been enough and he had vowed to stay dry. Disappointment was today. But disappointment could be beaten. It was only going to take sixty-one days.

"Trevithick is waiting in the car. I thought you might need this first."

"Thanks," he said and took hold of the cup. It had cooled a little in the five-minutes since she had made it and he took a welcome sip.

"So where were you?"

"Looking for Sarah," he paused. "Searching for answers in a bottle…"

"Did you find either?"

"No."

She nodded. "Any kind of timescale?"

"I searched for Sarah at the house. Then I came back here. I went to the new nursing home where her mother checked in as a resident yesterday. She wasn't there either. I don't know her address, gave up and got back here just after mid-night."

"No alibi?"

"There never is, is there?" he smiled knowingly. "What is happening at Malforth Manor? Late night, I take it."

"There's a fire-rescue unit working at the cave. We've drafted in a mountain and cave rescue unit from Wales, but they only got on the scene around four this morning."

"You're wasting your time," he said coldly. "Gowndry was under the rock. There were tonnes of it. It's a body-recovery operation. Nothing more."

"Well what should we do? Say a few prayers and lay a wreath? We still retrieve bodies and have a funeral, even in darkest Cornwall," she said, somewhat mockingly. "And while there's a body

275

unaccounted for, we treat it as a rescue until we know otherwise."

O'Bryan shrugged. "Well in that case, tell them to talk to Lucinda Ogilvy and find out where the entrance to the cave is through the house. It was bricked-up, but they should be three-hundred metres closer if they start at the other end."

She nodded, took out her phone and started to text. "I'm passing that on to the lead officer," she said. "Could have done with that information last night."

"Well, nobody thought to question me." He drank down half the cup then put it down decisively and nodded at her. "Let's go then."

They walked out to the car, where Trevithick was waiting. He was smoking a cigarette and looked impatient. He flicked the stub into the flowerbed and opened the driver's door. "Get in," he said.

"No, I'll follow you in mine."

"Are you not still over the limit?" he asked callously. "You looked to have had a skin full last night."

"You got a breathalyser?"

"I can send for one."

"I thought you were in a rush?"

He seemed to consider this for a moment, then said, "Alright, so be it. There'll be an officer at the crime scene with one, I'm sure."

"Okay, let's go then," O'Bryan said and unlocked his car. He was feeling self-destructive. One day it would get the better of him. That's what his shrink had kept telling him. he had fired him, was yet to get a second opinion. He got in, started up and waited for Trevithick and Hosking to get into their car.

The sky started to grey and by the time they drove out of Barlooe and through Point Geddon, the clouds were almost black. The rain started soon after and came down in sheets. O'Bryan had the wipers working at maximum but it wasn't nearly enough. He slowed down, reacting to Trevithick's change of pace, and he dropped back a little more than he usually would. The edges of the road ran like filthy muddy rivers, and the surface water was an inch deep. As they drove through a village called Carnon Downs the covers had blown off storm drains and geysers of brown water sprang at least two-feet into the air.

Trevithick drove a complicated route of narrow backroads and the roads dipped down through two separate valleys. O'Bryan followed carefully, and realised from the map on the satnav, and the signs on the road, that they were going to cross the river by ferry and head onto The Roseland Peninsular.

The rain ceased as abruptly as it had started. The clouds remained as grey and heavy and as threatening as they had been before the rainfall, and the landscape fell into a monochrome print. Although

277

the trees were still full with leaves, it looked like a stark winter's day. O'Bryan wondered what a dark February would look like in parts of Cornwall. Part of him hoped he'd never be there to see it.

O'Bryan pulled his car over into the painted waiting lane and watched the ferry make its way slowly across the river. The ferry was asymmetrical, with a folded squared-off ramp hoisted at either end. Through his steamed-up windscreen he could see the giant chains coming out of the water, threading through great cogs and sprockets. There was an audible clatter, which increased greatly as he lowered his steaming window. The air temperature was still fairly warm for late summer, and combined with the recent deluge of rain, the air steamed and smelled of damp and rotted vegetation. He increased the blowers on the windscreen and the mist cleared quickly. The ferry hit the concrete slipway and the ramp lowered with a mechanical whine. The crew of three worked efficiently and the cars started to disembark and negotiate the steep hill and sharp corner. In a matter of minutes, the queue edged forwards and started up the ramp. O'Bryan was waved forward right up to the bumper of the car in front. He was level with DCI Trevithick and DS Hosking. The ramp was raised and the ferry started on its ten-minute journey across the river. A crew member approached the window with an old fashioned ticket dispenser and a leather satchel and O'Bryan paid for a return ticket. He glanced at

Trevithick and the man looked away. O'Bryan opened his door and got out. He had noticed a viewing platform and stairs and thought he'd take a look at the river. The stairs were steel grate and echoed as he climbed them. He saw on old man leaning over the railings and smiled when he realised it was a dummy dressed like a pirate or smuggler. He walked past and leaned on the railings. He could see the river opening up on one side and two enormous cargo vessels on the other.

"They keep ships up here that need work." He turned and saw DS Hosking just a few feet away. "That, or when the crew have difficulties to resolve. A ship stayed here for three months because of some kind of industrial action. Another because the company could not pay the port fees."

O'Bryan nodded. "Must be deep."

"One of the deepest channels in the world. I think Falmouth is the deepest natural harbour. Or second deepest," she paused. "Shit, it's pretty deep, whatever…"

O'Bryan chuckled. "So that's the Carrick Roads, out there?" He pointed to the widening river.

"Yes."

"So the Pandora Inn is down that way?"

She nodded, stepped in closer and leaned against the railing next to him. "It's down that way, then back up another creek. There's a quite few creeks on the water."

"Trevithick still doesn't like me much, does he," he stated flatly. "He thinks I've killed Pete Mitchell."

"No," she paused. "He doesn't like you, no. But he doesn't think you killed Mitchell."

O'Bryan relaxed a little. He looked up and saw how close they were to the slipway. The water looked black and unimaginably deep, the sky was still as foreboding though and threatened to empty itself imminently. He realised they were almost across the river and said, "We'd better be getting back," he said.

The ramp scraped the concrete slipway and the gates opened. The cars had all long since started their engines and when the crew member started to wave the lanes of vehicles off it was like the start of a race. O'Bryan took his cue and left the ferry. Trevithick was now behind him and he drove a way up the steep road, then pulled in and waited for him to pass. Once he had, O'Bryan tucked in behind and followed him out of the valley. The road was fast, but most Cornish roads seemed to be. The traffic kept to ten miles an hour slower than a three lane motorway, but on a road with only a car and a half's width at most times. Pull ins had been cut into the hedges every fifty or sixty metres, so Cornish drivers would no doubt be adept at reversing as well as Le Mans racing.

They followed the road to Gerrans and Portscatho, but turned off shortly before. The road became even narrower and before long O'Bryan caught a glimpse of the sea. It was difficult to tell the blackness of the sea from the sky. The road dropped downhill and swept to the right. There was a slipway for launching small boats on the left and a sandy carpark on the right. Two police cars were parked as a barrier with one police officer sitting in one of the vehicles talking on the radio and three police officers milling around and chatting. They seemed to jump to it when they saw DCI Trevithick, but it was an isolated posting on a quiet morning. There was only so much busy that could be done. Before the two cars parked, they had reverted to chatting amongst themselves.

Large boulders lay scattered on the beach and the first third of the beach was made up almost entirely from pebbles and rocks, then gradually it turned to sand all the way down to the low-tide mark.

O'Bryan parked alongside Trevithick and got out of the Alfa Romeo. He looked at DS Hosking as she got out. She shivered, but it wasn't cold. She saw him looking and said, "I don't like this place much," she paused. "There were three fishermen gunned down here one night, a while ago. A smuggling venture gone wrong."

"Or gone right," O'Bryan said. "Depending on your point of view. It obviously worked out for someone."

"You've got all the smart answers, haven't you," Trevithick sneered. He pulled on an anorak over his suit. It wasn't raining, but it was merely a matter of time. "Come on." He strode out across the sandy carpark and headed for the police officers stationed on the road.

O'Bryan was surprised at the speed at which the detective walked. DS Hosking started to jog alongside. "No, he definitely still doesn't like you," she whispered.

Trevithick spoke to the uniformed officers briefly, nodded, then looked back at them as they approached. "SOCO are on the way to do a preliminary. They'll be here before mid-tide," he paused. "Before it's a problem, at least. This way," he said curtly.

O'Bryan looked out to sea. There was a thin sliver of grey between the blackness of the sky and the blackness mirrored by the Atlantic. White horses tossed all the way to the horizon. There were only three fishing vessels several miles out. Nobody went to sea on days like these unless their livelihoods depended on it. The beach was deserted. There was no real colour to it, merely the complete spectrum of grey in this monochrome scene. The rain started up again, heavy but by no means like the earlier deluge.

O'Bryan saw the pile of red in the middle of the beach. The colour emphasised by both the darkness of the sky and the sea and the emptiness of the waterlogged beach. His mind took a moment to take it in, then the realisation dawned. He jumped down off the ledge and onto the pebbles. Running on them was difficult, but it became easier as the terrain went through to shale and then wet sand. His heart raced, but only from knowing what he would find, and not from uncertainty or hope. The red gave way to pale skin tones and the long locks of amber hair, wet and matted, draped over her shoulders and the wet sand.

He slowed, walked the last few paces. Sarah stared blankly at him. Her eyes, once glossy and alert, looked dull and indifferent. Her skin had always been pale, but had now whitened and shone with a sheen of seawater. Her red dress was soaked, becoming almost see through, but even from where he stood, O'Bryan could see she wore no underwear underneath. He had snatched glimpses of a red bra under her dress last night.

He looked at both Hosking and Trevithick as they approached. "Has anybody disturbed the body?"

"It's been in the sea," Trevithick said. "There won't be any DNA."

"*She*, not it," O'Bryan corrected him.

"There could still be DNA internally," DS Hosking commented. "If anybody… interfered with her."

O'Bryan glanced down at Sarah's body, then looked back at DCI Trevithick. "I thought you wanted to speak to me regarding Pete Mitchell…"

Trevithick shrugged. "Don't know where you got that idea."

"So where *is* Pete Mitchell?"

"No idea," Trevithick paused. "But it looks like he left a little parting gift for you. Turn her over…"

"Why?" O'Bryan asked.

Trevithick stared at him, nodded towards the body. "Just do it."

"I'm not falling for it," O'Bryan said coldly. "I'm not touching a body after you asked me for an alibi for last night…"

"You're not under suspicion," DS Hosking interjected.

"So why the hell bring me out here? You inferred the body would be Mitchell's. You asked me for an alibi. What sort of crap are you peddling here?"

"Fine! I'll do it!" Trevithick bent down and grabbed hold of a handful of her red hair and pulled. He put his toe under her shoulder to lever her up.

O'Bryan kicked Trevithick in his buttocks, as much as a shove as a kick, and the man went sprawling into the wet sand. "Show some fucking respect!" he snapped. He knelt down in the sand and carefully eased his left hand under her waist and his right hand under her shoulder. She was ice cold, wet and sandy. Rigor mortis was starting to set in. There was a finality to it, more so than just seeing her body and knowing she was dead. It was a macabre confirmation. He eased her over into the recovery position, her head did not flop back when he let her go, she was stiffening quickly. He stood back and stared at her bare back. He took in the tiny dolphin tattoo he had seen, found somewhat erotic, when she had turned up with the takeaway.

"You see?" Trevithick said from behind him. He brushed the sand off his clothes and stood back. He didn't look happy, but he didn't square up to O'Bryan either. He seemed to take the fall, but he seemed smug too, like he was looking forward to something else to come. "You see what coming down here and poking about has done, where it has got you?"

The bleeding had long-since stopped and the sea had washed any blood away. The knife wounds were deep, cut at least an inch into her pallor flesh, the red of the muscle exposed and looking like veal steaks. O'Bryan had no trouble reading the message. He felt bile rise in his throat as he read.

O'Bryan - she's all yours now.

"So, why did you bring me out here?" O'Bryan asked quietly, staring at the words etched deep into her body. "You could have told me this back at the house."

Trevithick sneered at him. "You come down here, telling us what to do, with no authority and a letter you forged, just to give you credibility. Some hot-shit anti-terrorism officer with a medal you didn't deserve. Everybody knows you drowned that terrorist, even if it couldn't be proved…" he paused, his sneer turning to a look of pure loathing. "You treat me like some fucking security guard, not a DCI with twenty-years on the job. Well, here it is. This is what happened because you stirred up a load of shit and…"

He didn't finish the sentence. And nor did he see the punch coming. He was out cold and heading towards the sand. O'Bryan was already on him and grabbed him by his throat with his left hand and punched him twice more in the face with short, sharp jabs with his right fist. He pushed himself up and looked across at Hosking, who stared on, her mouth wide open. She looked at him, but said nothing. Trevithick was out cold and his mouth and nose were bleeding. O'Bryan turned and made his way back across the sand, and called without looking back, "Turn that piece of shit over before he becomes the second body on this shitty beach."

36

O'Bryan had driven to Camborne police station and found DS Harris in the CID suite. The detective sergeant had called social services and located the family for him. They were Syrian and their family name was Nassir. They had travelled for eleven months and lost the maternal grandmother on the way to a harsh winter and chronic asthma. They had what was left of their savings stolen in France. They had been approached in Calais and offered safe passage to England in return for work. In return for this, they were to be obligated for three months, then given jobs and paid in accordance to British law. It seemed like a good deal. They had been promised agricultural work. Maybe they would have, and maybe their lives would have been better for it. But that wasn't what happened to the Elmaleh family. Their story had been very different indeed, and O'Bryan knew that the Nassir's would not have been treated any differently. Especially as the family identified the criminal record photograph that O'Bryan had showed them as Pete Mitchell, the man who had approached them in Calais, and one of the men who had transported them across the channel, down the south coast of England and all the way up the creek to the jetty opposite Barlooe. O'Bryan had printed off a photograph from John Pascoe's social media account and the family had identified him as the second man on the boat.

They had been lucky, and they showed their gratitude in a series of hugs and thanks, from broken English spoken by the parents, to the middle-eastern Disney of the daughters. O'Bryan had been quite overwhelmed at their sincerity and appreciation. He had bid them farewell, then driven on to Truro.

He had wanted to deliver the news of Sarah's death to her mother. He hadn't wanted DS Hosking, with her judgemental views of the woman, nor DCI Trevithick to be the bearers. He had not known Sarah for very long, but he felt he had a connection. He had liked her, been attracted to her, and when he had discovered her story, her reasoning for what she had been forced to do, he had helped her all he could. But ultimately, he wanted to be the one to tell, because he had not been there for her at the end. He had asked her to wait outside of Ogilvy's study and that had been the last time he had seen her alive. He needed a penance. He needed to make amends. The ninth step. His path through alcohol recovery had been unchallenged at this step, this essential part of the process. He was starting on the road again, surely the final time, and he needed to take every single step this time. The ninth was the hardest of all. Had he not turned to the bottle after last night at Malforth Manor, he may well have found Sarah. May have been able to save her.

Emily Penhaligan had not taken the news well. She had yet to settle into the new residential home. Now there was grief and disbelief at the news, as well as the uncertainty of her new surroundings. He had spent an hour with her, hearing stories about Sarah's childhood, passing tissues, comforting her and explaining that the end had been swift. He knew, of course, that it hadn't been. It had been anything but. He could see for himself that her underwear had been removed and that it was likely Mitchell had raped her. It was more than likely she had been alive when the words had been cut into her, because drowning was Mitchell's proven method of killing. He suspected that the same method had been used to drown her as the entire Elmaleh family. Mitchell would have chosen the beach after rounding St Anthony Head on the Roseland Peninsular, as he escaped in his fishing vessel. He could be anywhere now, berthed in a quiet cove or creek, or perhaps even in France. He would have a knowledge of the French coastline if he had successfully brought in illegal immigrants.

O'Bryan had looked for a carer to sit with Emily and taken his leave. He felt awful. Awful enough for a drink? No doubt. But today was day one, and he was sure he would make it this time.

He had packed his bag and dropped it in the doorway to the lounge. He would have to give the keys back to Anderson's wife when he returned to London. There would be the funeral too. It suddenly struck him that in the whirlwind since finding out about Anderson's battle with cancer and his death, and watching the boat moor on the jetty across the creek, he had not had a moment to grieve. Maybe Anderson would have wanted it like that. Perhaps that was why he had sent O'Bryan down under the guise of recovery, then sent him the file. O'Bryan certainly liked the thought of that.

He picked up his jacket, then frowned at the weight. The pocket. He fished out the mobile phone. John Pascoe's mobile phone. There was little battery left, but the screen indicated a number of missed calls and texts. O'Bryan thumbed through as he made his way to his bag and took his charger out of the side pocket. He wanted to get some charge into it before it switched off. It was an iPhone, and many were set up to require a thumbprint upon restarting. Pascoe hadn't had a screen lock code installed, but even so, everyone set up their phone differently.

Plugged in and charging, O'Bryan looked at the numbers, the names and the times and dates of the calls and texts. He looked at the screen thoughtfully, then started to compose a reply to the last text it had received.

37

O'Bryan watched the car turn a wide circle, its headlights cutting a swathe of light through the darkness like a lighthouse through a thick sea-mist. The driver parked up nose out. It was a professional thing to do. You could get out of trouble faster that way.

O'Bryan had driven up earlier, parked in a field after battling to open the gate. His car was next to the hedge, unseen from the track. He hadn't responded to the text. He had bait on the hook and a nibble had been taken. He needed to tease until he got a real bite. In this case, doing nothing was everything.

The driver switched off the engine and the lights went out after thirty-seconds. Courtesy lights to get you into your house. O'Bryan remained where he was. He watched, waited. The car was parked twenty-feet from the edge of the abyss. Nobody goes that close to the abyss without looking down at it. It was a morbid human fascination. Like the people who had parked and walked across the road at Hell's Mouth. O'Bryan had done the same. Sure enough, after a minute or so, the door opened and the driver got out. The half-moon illuminated them. O'Bryan made his move. He climbed up the hedge, swung his leg over and slid down. He pushed himself out from the hedge and stepped up out of the ditch. He was twenty-metres away.

"You should have moved the for rent sign," he said.

DS Becky Hosking spun around, squinted at him in the darkness, her eyes were not yet accustomed to the dark. "What do you mean? What are *you* doing here, Ross?"

"Back at that executive new-build in Porthtowan," he said. "The house had a for rent sign from Clive and Gowndry. The sign had been taken down and stored by the side of the house. The same estate agents as the house Sarah was working out of both in Point Geddon and Portreath. The same Clive Gowndry who was up to his neck in the illegal trafficking and imprisonment of people for the sex-slave trade."

"I just got the keys to that house to meet you somewhere safe and private," she said defensively.

"I went into more than just the bathroom," he paused. "There was a room geared up for accepting clients. It was a working brothel. You said the house was part of an investigation, but nothing had been tagged or logged. No evidence had been removed."

"You'll have to do better than that!" she scoffed. "What exactly are you accusing me of?"

"I don't buy that you had a call to get back to the station. I don't think you wrote me a note and I'm sure your phone records will prove there was never a call. So, what was meant to have happened? John

Pascoe enters the house as you leave and attacks me? Binds my hands and drives me up here?"

"What the hell has John Pascoe got to do with this?"

"You tell me," he said. "You're up here tonight because of the text from his phone."

"So?"

"He's the third man in this endeavour. He's a lawyer."

"And?"

"You had a lawyer boyfriend. You clashed in court. You said you left him because he got a man off a rape charge," O'Bryan said. "That man was Pete Mitchell. That lawyer was John Pascoe. I've checked. It isn't difficult to do."

"It's a small county. Coincidence is a daily occurrence."

"I asked around, spoke to some of your team. DS Harris in particular. He said you and John Pascoe were still very much an on and off item."

"Fuck buddy, so what?" she said flippantly. "I'm up here responding to his text. A woman has needs."

"Pascoe was up to his neck in all of this. He has been identified as one of the men who brought the Nassir's into the country. His work schedule will confirm he was absent at the time. I bet that it will do the same around the time of the Elmaleh family's deaths. I'm also willing to bet he was stupid enough to carry his mobile phone at the time. It's as good as a tracking device."

"Like I said, coincidence."

"When we went back to Camborne's CID suite for you to sort out the request for the exhumation, you were being really *friendly* with me."

"It was a friendly kind of day!" She smiled, cocked her head. "I seem to remember you asking for a date."

O'Bryan shrugged. "I do a lot that I later regret," he paused. "DS Harris slipped his jacket on and left abruptly. I thought he was pissed off that you were helping the stranger in the camp, that he was loyal to DCI Trevithick. He just thought you were working another angle. He is in line for detective inspector, as are you. As usual, there's two qualified officers, but only one post. He feels that you have an unfair advantage. It would appear that you are the golden girl. Not because of your abilities as a police officer. But because of your on and off, two-year affair with DCI Trevithick. Nobody's meant to know, but like most offices, everybody does."

"It happens. You end up working a lot of hours, the same hours…"

"I thought Trevithick was involved. I thought that he blocked Pengelly, Adams and Harris and called for no further action. You had the man's ear. Not only did he want to continue massaging both his ego and other things with a younger, attractive woman, he was desperate for his wife not to find out about his affair. He has two young teens, doesn't want his family pulled apart. You were his puppeteer, through nothing more than sex and a few calculated, but casual-sounding conversations on how it could pan out for him if he didn't listen to you. You controlled him, and with that, the angle from within the police. Guided by Pascoe, or maybe you guided him…" He shook his head. "No, I know you guided him. *Guided* them all. You played me too, all the little flirtations, I was just a fool to believe you would be interested. And today, on the beach, Trevithick said that there would be no DNA after exposure to the seawater, but it was *you* who said that it could still be there internally. That was the whole reason for digging up the Elmaleh family. You felt that if it were looked into, which would only be a matter of time, then the DNA of whoever had sex with them… *raped* them, would create a trail. Sooner or later there would be a match and it would all come crashing down. You got lucky with the racial tension thing, the Islamic community insisting they were properly buried. It made an open and shut case shut far more quickly."

She shrugged. "So now what? Are you recording this?"

He shook his head. "No. Not this time."

"So what do you want? Money?" she asked. "Everyone want's money."

"Not everyone."

"Then they're stupid. There's more than enough money to change your life forever. I can get you a quarter of a million tonight. Just to keep quiet and walk away. Think about it; that's a hell of an amount of money. If you want in, you could take on a role from London. There's dirty immigrants on every street up there. They're all over the place. You could send them down our way. You could earn that much again in another three months. A million a year, no problem. I have, and I've stashed it away." She looked at him curiously. "How did you get John's phone?"

"You followed him when he drove me up here, didn't you," he said accusingly. "You took him back for his car."

"I knew he'd pussy out," she said. "I should have stayed and helped him. You cut him a deal, didn't you? Spineless piece of shit. They're all the same, lawyers. So what, will he turn Queen's evidence? Cut a deal for immunity?"

"There was no deal."

"So where did he get to?"

O'Bryan stepped closer to her and she stepped back a pace. She was no more than four-feet from the edge. "He was going to get me into my car and send it over the edge. You planned it with him. You helped him by driving him back for his car. So what? You didn't want to get your own hands dirty?"

296

"That bastard," she said coldly. "So he confessed and gave you the phone. Then what?"

O'Bryan tossed her Pascoe's phone and she caught it. It was reactionary and she looked at the screen. He shook his head. "No. He took my place," he said. "After I killed him, kicked the life out of him, I strapped him into his Porsche and gave it a little bump over the edge with my car."

"You *killed* him?" she looked at him disbelievingly. "Bullshit! You wouldn't do that…"

"You don't know me at all."

"Oh, I think I do," she sneered. "You're a fucking boy scout! You're all about what's right and wrong!"

"I'm all about sticking up for people who can't. I'm all about justice, yes."

"So you did drown that terrorist…"

He nodded. "One less to worry about."

She cocked her head and stared incredulously. "Seriously, you killed John Pascoe?"

"He's right below you."

She looked like she did not know whether to laugh or cry. "You murdered him! Well, that ties you in now, we're both the wrong side of the law," she said, then smiled. "Well perhaps now, we cancel each other out…"

O'Bryan took a quick step forwards and shoved her hard in her chest. She staggered backwards, her face not comprehending what he had done, but as her feet found no purchase and she reached the edge, her eyes went wide and she started to scream. The scream lasted an agonising four seconds before silence followed. Ominous and final.

38

Five days later
London

O'Bryan wasn't a lover of religion, but he would have to admit that he found churches to be a calm, contemplative place to spend time. There was a serenity that he found difficult to describe. The same went with graveyards. Perhaps there was an acceptance that eventually, even if you lived your life without religion, you ended up somewhere like this. The proximity to death made one contemplate life, and while doing so, with the knowledge that we are here for such a short time, serenity is easily reached. It wasn't something you could fight against and win. Ultimately, there really was only one conclusion for all.

The graveyard was neatly kept, the grass cut short and the bushes and shrubs trimmed and shaped to keep the path free for people to walk two-abreast, as was common practice when walking to burial plots, behind a coffin carried by six.

He had missed the funeral. He had at least wanted to hear Anderson's eulogy, but he had been assured by those he knew in attendance that it was both fitting and bullshit. A parody that so many knew so little about the man, and so few knew little more. There were anecdotes told that his colleagues knew nothing of, and untold anecdotes his colleagues dare not divulge to his family. A life of almost thirty-years in the police, with twenty of those years spent in the fight against terrorism had left its mark. Anderson was both a larger than life character and a shadow, depending on who you asked.

The investigation into DS Hosking's involvement with John Pascoe was ongoing. Quite how or why events had led them both to the precipice was unclear. Their bodies had been recovered. Hosking's at nearby Porthtowan, further up the tidal current and Pascoe's car had been spotted by an ornithologist at low tide. Just enough shadow for the man, familiar to the location to know there was an anomaly. A search and rescue team had recovered his body, but as yet any recovery of the vehicle looked unlikely. Phone records had shown multiple texts and calls between Hosking and Pascoe. Officers had been drafted down from Exeter to lead and DCI Trevithick had been suspended pending an internal enquiry. Pete Mitchell was still at large and subject to an active UK manhunt as well as on Interpol's watch list.

O'Bryan hadn't brought flowers with him. He imagined there would have been enough already, and besides, Anderson would have ribbed him terribly about giving another man flowers. He had found the grave easily enough. Freshly dug and filled with loose earth piled in a slight mound, the headstone newly polished and seated perfectly upright. The headstone was, however, non-descript. There were black marble affairs, with white or gold inlaid writing, that seemed to be a popular choice, but either Anderson had left instructions, or his wife had chosen an austere stone that looked like slate to O'Bryan. The engraving was deep and in a relatively plain font. Nothing flamboyant, nothing to indicate that a good man rested here, a man who had gone over and above for the security of his country.

O'Bryan sat back on the bench. The trees were starting to shed their leaves and even though he was only three-hundred miles east and a hundred miles north of Cornwall, he felt a chill upon returning. The summer was finally over and like so many things in his life, he would be glad to lay it to rest and move on.

"Are you here for Commander Anderson?" The voice belonged to a man, but was unduly quiet.

In his respectful, sombre state, O'Bryan had been startled by the voice behind him and flinched. He turned and saw a gentle-looking man in his fifties. He wore a dog collar and a black shirt. Anderson had been Church of England so this would make the man a vicar, or at least O'Bryan assumed so. "I have," he said. "I missed the ceremony…"

"Funeral, my son," the vicar smiled. "Ceremonies are for weddings…" There was no condescension in his tone.

"Fair enough."

"Are you a family member? I could say a few words if you'd like?"

O'Bryan shook his head. "No, I'm not. And no, that's okay, thanks."

"A colleague?"

"Yes."

"And a member?"

O'Bryan frowned. "Sorry?"

"Not member, no. I mean a fellow brother."

"Brother?"

"Yes," the vicar said. "There was a good showing, a little ceremony afterwards from his brothers at the lodge." He looked at O'Bryan, then added, "The freemasons…"

O'Bryan got up off the bench and walked over to the grave. He looked at the headstone. At the top, in the centre of the stone, above the name was an emblem, an insignia. A set-square and compass, centred over a letter F within a globe. There were no accompanying words. It was small and he had mistaken it for a rose or something similar.

O'Bryan thought about what Sarah had said about John Pascoe. A freemason from a family of freemasons. Clive Gowndry's handshake. O'Bryan had confronted him about it, taunted him even, in Malforth Manor at the charity event.

Had Anderson known? Had they approached him, a fellow mason? Asked him to help them in their sickening endeavour? What had sparked Anderson to have his inkling about the deaths of the Elmaleh family? How did he know there was going to be more? He had marked the dates and times of the high tides for O'Bryan to keep a lookout. And why had he not briefed O'Bryan thoroughly, given him a clear path to follow, rather than instructions to start at the beginning and see what he could turn up? Would he have felt torn between justice and the idea of turning against his fellow brethren?

Tell me when you see it…

Those had been Anderson's final words to O'Bryan.

O'Bryan looked down at the headstone. He had a lump in his throat and a tear was welling in his eye and he said quietly, "I see it now…"

Author's Note

Thanks for making it this far and I hope you enjoyed reading the story as much as I enjoyed writing it.

This story marks a new direction. It's always exciting to create a new character and I think DCI Ross O'Bryan has much to give. There's a dark past in there, but a true heart. He's flawed, possibly because the best people always are, but from rock bottom comes the will to battle on and show true strength and I plan more outings for him soon.

That's not to say previous series are over. Far from it. I have left Rob Stone hanging at the border to Alaska with half the FBI on his tail and few options ahead of him, while Alex King seems to have it all at his feet – a new love, career and a life ahead of him, with the killing in his past. Oh, how we writers can pull the rug from under our characters at any minute... I'm working on more of these stories and these guys have had it easy so far!

There are links at the front of the book if you would like to connect with me and know more about what I'm writing, when the next book is out and other related topics – thanks for reading once again and I hope to entertain you soon!

A P Bateman

Also by A P Bateman

The Ares Virus

At a US research facility funded by the military and clandestine agencies a super-virus has been created as a first strike military weapon. During its conception the anti-virus has furthered the possibilities of medical research by decades. Such is its potential, treachery has struck from within. If the virus is released, then the anti-virus will be worth billions to the pharmaceutical industry. Isobel Bartlett worked on the project and knows its potential.

After the suspicious death of her mentor, and upon hearing part of an audacious plan to make money from the project she flees the facility with the information needed to culture the viruses to seek help from a contact with the FBI. Up against rogue government forces, she is helped by Agent Rob Stone of the Secret Service who has been tasked by the president to investigate a disbanded assassination program after his investigation led him to the bio research facility. The two are hunted mercilessly by an assassin from Washington to the streets of New York. Only when the hunt reaches the wild forests of Vermont can ex-special forces soldier Stone take the fight to the enemy.

The Contract Man

When an MI6 agent is found to be keeping records of his missions to protect himself from betrayal he unwittingly makes himself a priority target. But how do you silence the most dangerous man imaginable? Send him into hell on earth…

While Alex King is sent into Northern Iraq to tidy the loose ends of a botched mission, the archipelago of Indonesia is under communist threat from within its own military. A consortium of worried businessmen call for desperate measures and seek the services of an assassin. But what if MI6 could be duped into taking care of their problems for them? With secret links to China the communist contingent threatens Britain's trade initiatives with the largest mineral producing country on the planet.

In the dark world of intelligence, it seems that everybody has their price.

Lies and Retribution

MI5 agents have been executed and more agents have been abducted with no terms received from the kidnappers. An MI5 analyst is missing having accessed and downloaded prohibited security data.

The trial of notorious radical cleric Mullah Al-Shaqqaf collapses, his extradition falls apart. A man known to have funded ISIS, recruit fighters for Syria and coerce teenagers to martyr themselves. Again he walks free.

The hunt for a nuclear warhead stolen ten years ago has led Russian intelligence to London.
One man connects them all…

When retired MI6 operative Alex King is contacted by the deputy director of MI5 with a proposition, he feels compelled to act. His brief is illegal, his actions unprecedented. The law and the courts have failed. Time and events are against the nation's intelligence services and the battle can no longer be fought by the rules. Britain's enemies will soon find the game has changed.

As MI5 agent Caroline Darby investigates with the help of a seasoned Scotland Yard detective she soon starts to look through the elaborate misdirection and discovers the horrifying truth…

The Town

Rob Stone is taking time out to climb in the mountains of Oregon. Taking a break, drinking coffee in a diner in a small mountain town he watches a helpless man humiliated. Stepping in to help, he sparks a confrontation. Within an hour somebody tries to kill him.

A message has been sent, but Stone will not be pushed. As he starts to investigate what some people in the town do not want uncovered, the truth becomes unthinkable. Cruelty on a scale unimaginable, Stone is determined to shut it down and reclaim the town for its people.

Outnumbered, hunted through the dense forest and mountain terrain, his enemy are unaware that they haven't gained the advantage. They have merely released him into his element.

Murder… Abduction… Betrayal… Sometimes you can't see the woods for the trees…

The Island

Waking naked and alone on a deserted island, Rob Stone has no recollection of how he got there, or who he is. His memory is one of snapshots, each one building a picture of what he does and who he truly is.

He discovers he has both the skills and will to survive. But survival is one thing, being hunted is another.

A beautiful journalist in desperate need of help. The dark web, the dumping ground for the evil of the internet. An enemy from his past. Murder, abduction and betrayal. Stone must try to remember the time before the island changed everything. The island will help him remember. The island will make him wish he could forget.

When the unthinkable becomes reality…

Shadows of Good Friday

(An Alex King Prequel, set seventeen years before
The Contract Man)
In the last days before signing the peace agreement,
an IRA splinter cell mounts an operation on the
British mainland using English criminals. This
unprecedented move intrigues MI6 and they assume
command of MI5's surveillance operation.

A career criminal is released from prison and
aims to win back the wife and child his sentence has
cost him, but before he can, he is forced back into his
old world. The stakes have changed and his family
have become leverage for the most ruthless people
imaginable.

A woman imprisoned in an abusive
relationship, desperate to escape with her son and
rekindle her past becomes the pawn in a deadly world
of deception, violence and retribution.

A clandestine wing of the secret intelligence
service tests its newest recruit. Alex King has trained
and operated in the shadowy world of intelligence and
now he must kill for his country, but before he can, he
needs to discover more about the men he has been
sent to kill.

Made in the USA
Columbia, SC
08 September 2017